EGGNOG, EXTORTION, & EVERGREENS

A Camper And Criminals Cozy Mystery

Book Fourteen

BY
TONYA KAPPES

TONYA KAPPES
WEEKLY NEWSLETTER

Want a behind-the-scenes journey of me as a writer?
The ups and downs, new deals, book sales, giveaways and more? I share it all! Join the exclusive Southern Sleuths private group today! Go to www.patreon.com/Tonyakappesbooks

As a special thank you for joining, you'll get an exclusive copy of my cross-over short story, *A CHARMING BLEND.* Go to Tonyakappes.com and click on subscribe at the top of the home page.

"We better not get caught." The woman's voice cracked.

"Who's going to know? Visiting hours are over, with us being the one exception. And that girl next door is as dead as he is, only they are dragging out her death."

Wait. Was he referring to me?

"Hello." There was a different voice. "How's Mr. Lenz tonight?"

"No change. Do you think he'll come out of this?" The woman and man were stopped from smothering the poor patient.

"Rest assured we are trying everything in our power to make sure he does." There was a little fiddling in the background that sounded like the nurse was clicking away on a keyboard and maybe checking his vitals. "His oxygen level is a little low, but with the ventilator, it'll help keep those levels up. I see by his chart that his kidney function is still good. I'll be back in to check on you."

There was a long pause. I strained to hear anything more, but the couple had gone eerily quiet.

Then came the sound that everyone knew because it was on all the hospital shows when someone died: the short beeps followed by a long and drawn-out beep that led to a flurry of activity before the zing of the curtains cut through.

"Randy? Randy?" the woman cried out. "Oh no. I think he. . ." her voice faltered.

There was a lot of chatter going on from various people I didn't recognize.

"Is he dead?" the man asked with a concerned tone.

"I'm sorry." There was a male's voice that apologized. "I'm afraid we couldn't save him this time."

The woman, who I recognized as one of the whisperers, cried out, "No. No. No," followed by sobs.

"Now, now, honey. He's in a much better place now." The man was trying to comfort her.

"You're acting!" my voice escaped from my lips as my eyes flew open. "You murderer!" I flung up to sitting and gasped for breath.

The curtain zipped open between me and a few people I didn't recognize.

"Mae, you're awake."

CHAPTER ONE

"Oh, Mae. Oh, Mae." Hank's voice quivered. "Please open your eyes."

I'm here. I'm here, I could hear myself think.

"It's just me and you. Squeeze my hand." I felt his warm hand over mine. "Come on, baby. Squeeze it now, Mae." The tone of his voice quickly faded from desperation to commanding with a hint of anger.

I am squeezing. I am trying. My thoughts drifted off. Why couldn't I see or talk? Where was I?

I drowned out Hank's pleas and listened to the darkness that surrounded me. There were the shuffling of feet, the creak of wheels like a cart zooming past, beeps upon beeps echoing near and far, but I wasn't clear as to what was happening. The sound of a something being zipped caught my attention.

"Anything?" An unfamiliar woman's voice brought me back to Hank.

"No. Just laying here." There was a faint wisp of air across my cheek as his hand pulled away from mine. "I'll move."

"It's okay." The woman had a comforting voice. "Do they know how long she was in the car?"

"No. They don't even think anyone saw her car until I went looking for her." He gave me a clue.

Car? I was in a car?

"All of her vital signs are good. I'm sure she's just unconscious from hitting her head on the steering wheel." The woman's cold hands touched my wrist. There was a moment of pause. "Her heart rate is good. She doesn't have a fever."

"When will the results of her CAT scan come in about her brain?" Hank's question alarmed me.

My brain? CAT scan? Was I in a car wreck?

There was clicking that sounded like someone typing, which made me think I was in a hospital and the nurse was looking up something or recording my vitals she'd just taken.

"It looks like the results are in." Even though I was only able to hear her, I could tell she was offering a smile by the tone of her voice. "I'm sure the doctor will be right in."

"Can you just tell me if she's got brain damage?"

Brain damage? I inwardly laughed. *I'm here! I'm right in here!* my own voice screamed inside of my head.

"I'm not a radiologist and certainly not a doctor. I can only see the results have been posted." Her footsteps came a little closer. There was a brushing sound.

Was she rubbing Hank somewhere?

He sobbed. "Oh, Mae. Just open your eyes," Hank started to beg all over again. "I can't be without you. I only found you again for a couple of years."

"Oh, I'm sorry." She was comforting my boyfriend.

Get your hands off my boyfriend. If I am in a coma or whatever you want to call this crazy situation, I'm not dying, and I will hunt you down.

"Ahem." Someone cleared their throat, causing some shuffling of feet. "Well? Any change?" The gruff sound of Dottie Swaggert's voice popped into my ears.

Hank cleared his voice. He sniffled. "No. I was just talking to her." His voice went back to the normal big-and-bad detective tone he used when he was trying to be strong and brave. "Raye was telling me the brain scan results are posted."

"Raye?" Dottie's voice held sarcasm. "First-name basis?"

Dottie Swaggert was a spitfire. Though I couldn't see her with my eyes, I was visualizing her in my head, and I was sure she was wearing some sort of sweatshirt, a tight pair of jeans, and hiking boots, with her cigarette case in hand. I sure would love to see those pink curlers she snapped in her red hair, but as much as I tried to see, it was black.

What I would give for me and Dottie to be sitting in the Happy Trails Campground office right now having a big cup of coffee. Oh, and using the fresh beans from the Trails Coffee Shop.

My hearing began to fade as a memory of earlier flashed in my head like lightning.

CHAPTER TWO

S IX HOURS EARLIER
"Good afternoon," I greeted my friend when I walked into the Trails Coffee Shop located in downtown Normal, Kentucky. "There are so many cool vendors out there this year."

"Mm-hmm. You can only have so many pot holders and wooden ornaments with your name on them, and them homemade candles stink to high heaven." Mary Elizabeth Moberly, my foster mother, sat at one of the café tables inside of the coffee shop with a cup of the sweet-and-spicy-with-a-full-body blend that Gert Hobson had specially made for the fall season.

"You better take what I have left of the fall blend if you need some for the hospitality room, because I don't have much left, and we've been selling the Snowman Spice Christmas Blend." Gert shrugged when she went to refill my cup. "Which means you should grab some of that too."

She set an empty basket on our table and brushed off her coat that was covered in freshly fallen snow. "So far, it's the biggest seller at the Winter Festival."

Gert—as well as other local shop owners in Normal—and I had agreements we would promote each other's businesses. Since I owned Happy

Trails Campground, I loved to feature her coffee in the hospitality room for my camping guests to sample so they would go into town and visit her coffee shop. In turn, she would recommend Happy Trails Campground to tourists who were looking for a place to park their camper, tent camp, or even rent one of the many bungalow cabins. Plus, she kept my business cards and flyers on her corkboard. It was a win-win for all the merchants in our little town to promote each other, and we all did it for one another.

"I'll be sure to buy some before I leave." I tapped my phone, bringing it out of sleep mode to check the time. "Which will be soon. I'm expecting the new campers to be checking in shortly."

Happy Trails Campground didn't have specific days tourists could come. Instead, we had specific times. For example, check-in was at three and checkout was at one in the afternoon.

Sundays were always a big day for people to check in because they liked to stay a week or two. With the Winter Festival in town and all the advertising the National Park Committee had been doing, the campground was full starting today.

"Wee doggie!" Dottie Swaggert had walked into the coffee shop with Betts Hager and Abby Fawn. All three of them headed over to our table. "It's colder than a mother-in-law's love out there."

She tossed her oversized coat, and it flopped across the other chair at the table along with her big scarf and her cross-body purse. Her orange knit cap was still pulled down over her hair with red strands sticking out.

"It is gorgeous, though." I couldn't help but look out over downtown Normal.

There was a large median that divided Main Street. On each side was a one-way going in the opposite direction of the other. The median was large enough to have an amphitheater at the far end with seating for seasonal theatrical shows as well as several picnic tables, plenty of grass, and large trees.

Since Normal was located in the heart of the Daniel Boone National Forest, we did anything and everything we could to keep the economy going since we were considered a tourist town for all things that included camping adventures.

Winter was always the hardest for getting tourists.

As the newest member of the local chapter of the National Parks Committee, I'd come up with a solution for the lack of tourists during the winter months so we didn't have to work so hard during the other seasons to stockpile our money.

I had suggested a Winter Festival where Kentucky artisans rented booths in the downtown area. We also opened some of the trails with the frozen cascades since the park would close them due to the slippery paths.

It took a lot of volunteers to stay on the trails and keep them clear of ice so tourists could make it to the cascades, which were gorgeous when they were frozen. Then the idea took on a life of its own. The citizens were completely into it—so much so that they'd named it Old-Fashion Camping Christmas.

Gert had come back with to-go cups and quickly filled them up with the coffee carafe.

"'Tis the season." Betts picked up her cup of coffee and held it in the air for us to toast.

Gert, Abby, Betts, Dottie, Mary Elizabeth, and I held our cups in the air.

"Ho ho ho." Bett's eyes glowed beneath her bangs. She let out a laugh and tossed her wavy brown hair over her shoulder.

"Hold that pose and smile." Abby Fawn raised her phone to take a selfie with all of us in it. She flung her head side to side and looked at herself to see which angle looked best on her.

"Pfft. Pfft." Dottie spit and waved her hand in front of her face, knocking away Abby's swinging ponytail that'd hit her in the mouth. "Watch where you swing that thing," Dottie snarled.

"Say 'snow'!" Abby smiled and clicked when we were all smiling at her phone. "Hashtag old-fashioned Christmas. Hashtag festival. Hashtag Normal, Kentucky." Abby typed away on her social media accounts.

"Honestly, you should drop the whole librarian and Tupperware gig and be a marketing strategist," Betts told Abby. Abby had established a social media following, and they had dubbed her the social media queen for all things hashtag Daniel Boone National Forest.

"Speaking of Tupperware, I have some great sales down at my booth, which"—she shoved her phone in her coat pocket—"I need to get back down to so that I can take orders."

"I've got to get back out to my booth too." Gert held up the carafe. "Anyone need a refill before I go?"

"Thank you. I'll take mine back to Happy Trails." I opened the lid and let her top me off.

"Are you sure you don't need any help?" Dottie asked. She was the campground manager and lived on the campground in her trailer, just a few lots down from my full-time camper.

"No." I shook my head and stood up, shrugging my winter coat on. "Just make sure you let me know what vendors we might be able to contact and use in the baskets."

I was always searching for new products to put in the different baskets we sold to our guests. Happy Trails Campground had several options for our guests. We had a full-site hookup with water and electricity for anyone who wanted to haul in their camper. We offered campers for them to rent, along with the bungalows, which were cabins of various sizes. We even offered tent lots for the die-hard earth campers but not during the winter.

Since I offered rentable campers, the campground had taken off. There'd been a lot of honeymoons, bridal parties, bachelor parties, and overall romantic getaways, to name a few. We also offered themed baskets as well.

Our two most popular were the spa breakfast baskets, which was why Gert was suggesting I grab what I needed.

"Good for us." Betts nudged Dottie and winked. "Ladies, our shopping awaits."

There was a slight groan that came from Mary Elizabeth. The last thing she wanted to do was buy anything homemade. She liked to go to fancy shops and purchase from a shelf, not from a card table like the rest of us.

"I'll see you later." She kissed me on the cheek. "We have to get the Christmas supper menu finalized." Her head tilted, and her brows rose, making her shoulder-length hair sway to the side, exposing her large pearl stud earrings, ones she never took out.

"Let's go, fancy pants." Dottie tugged on Mary Elizabeth's Lilly Pulitzer tapestry coat that cost more than my camper. "Is that a rug you've got wrapped around you?" Dottie, who caught life as it came and never took herself too seriously, joked, knowing that Mary Elizabeth wouldn't find it a bit funny.

"Ho, ho, ho." Dottie turned her attention to Hank Sharp when he walked into the door. "Mm-hmm, Mae." She slowly shook her head. "He sure is a fine-looking young man."

"Yes he is." My heart swooned as I watched my detective boyfriend walk into the coffee shop, stopping at the various groups of citizens and wishing them a Merry Christmas on his way over to me.

He looked at me. His green eyes twinkled like the lights on a Christmas tree against his black hair. The tip of his black turtleneck beneath his black buttoned-up coat just made him appear even more dapper.

"Ladies." He flashed them a smile when he greeted them. "Mae." My toes tingled when he said my name, and my heart jumped when he kissed me.

"Your lips are cold," I whispered and kissed him again.

"You can help warm them up over supper tonight at The Red Barn. Say around seven?" He was so good about taking me on dates still.

"You better believe it." My nose crinkled above my smile. "It's perfect timing, too, because I'm working in the office today."

"Good. I'll pick you up." He kissed me again before he headed up to the counter to get his order. "Granny sent me to get some Snowman coffee before it's all gone."

Hank's granny, Agnes, worked with him at the sheriff's department as the dispatcher.

"Wait." Gert stopped Hank when he turned around. "Take a couple of treats for Precious. And a few for Fifi and Chester."

Tourists loved to bring their furry friends camping. We'd seen an increase in types of pets they brought to Happy Trails. Dogs were a norm, but sometimes we'd get campers with cats and even birds. Yes, I'd had a camper who had a birdcage in her RV.

Each shop in downtown Normal allowed pets to come in. There were even water bowls along the sidewalk for them.

"Thank you, Gert." I took the bag of treats. "I'll go give them one before I start working."

"You be careful out there." Hank stood in front of me. He buttoned the top button of my coat. "Can't risk you getting a cold."

"Thank you, doctor," I teased and tried to stop the giddy smile from taking over my face.

"Seriously, the roads are getting slick." He pushed back a strand of my long curly hair. "Don't give me that look." His eyes narrowed. "I worry about you. The roads are curvy, and though you know them, these crazy tourists out there don't. We've had a lot of crash calls come in, and since there's not anything going on with my department, Jerry has me out on calls." By Jerry, he referred to Sheriff Jerry Truman. "The deputies are busy today. The snow is going to keep falling, and when the sun goes down, it'll all turn to ice."

"I get it. I'll be careful. Two hands on the wheel." I pushed up on the toes of my snow boots and gave him one more kiss. "Though I'd rather be right here with you, both of us have to go to work."

"Yeah, yeah. Come on, I'll walk you to your car." He gestured toward the door, where we were met with more tourists coming in to get a tasty treat.

"It's gorgeous here." I stopped on the sidewalk and took in the views.

There were white twinkling Christmas lights as far as the eye could see. The gaslights on the posts of the amphitheater glowed as the snow danced to the ground. There were large poinsettias scattered along the median. All the tree trunks were covered in lights, creating a true winter wonderland with tourists walking around the booths. Everyone had a big smile on their face as they talked to one another.

That was what made small campground towns so fun, especially southern ones where the hospitality far exceeded any other tourist town.

"The shops look so good." Hank pointed out all the little mom-and-pop shops on each side of the median. They were freestanding cottage-style homes with little side yards.

There were small shops that ran along each side of Main Street. They ranged from the Smelly Dog, which was a pet groomer, to Normal Diner, as well as the Tough Nickel Thrift Shop and Deter's Feed-N-Seed, along with more boutique-type shops that I couldn't wait to check out. The display windows of each shop even had visions of families camping and summers in Normal.

It was the side yards that sparkled for the festival. Even Alvin Deters, owner of Deter's Feed-N-Seed, had put a live Christmas tree in his side yard next to the snowmobile he was showcasing, along with a snowblower, snowplow, skis, snowboards, and other various things he sold during these winter months.

Ethel Biddle had the best and most popular display. She owned Smelly Dog and she'd had a small shed built in her side yard that was lattice all around like a miniature gingerbread house. Inside of the shed was a cozy little room with a pellet stove to warm by when you waited to sit on Santa's lap. Yep. Ethel had pulled the old Santa card. But she did it for a good cause. Since she really didn't have anything to sell to the tourists, all the money raised for having your photo taken with the jolly ole fellow went to the local SPCA, Society for the Prevention of Cruelty to Animals.

She'd even set up a small stage outside of the gingerbread house where Blue Ethel and the Adolescent Farm Boys, her own bluegrass band, played a few Christmas carols for strollers to enjoy.

Sweet Smell Flower Shop had the prettiest display. Of course, they'd used all the seasonal garlands and flowers along with the cutest Christmas decorations to entice tourists into their shop, where they were making special Christmas swags for campers. It was a super cute idea.

When I passed by the Laundry Club, the local laundromat and where Betts, Abby, Dottie, Queenie French, and I liked to hang out, I noticed Queenie was in there and alone.

"What? No last-minute Christmas shopping to do?" I'd popped my head in to check on her. "Or are you in here for Betts?"

"Betts had a big order coming in from the Bible-thumpers. They're having that big Christmas carol show with the snack at the undercroft after." There was a hint of dislike that crossed her face. "So I told Betts I'd just wait here for them to drop the tablecloths off and get them started since they kicked me out."

It wasn't that they kicked her out. Queenie French was the local Jazzercise instructor, and the Normal Baptist Church let her use the undercroft for free for her classes. The downside was in times like this, when they needed their space for themselves.

"Look at these machines all going." Queenie pushed the hunter-green headband up on her forehead, causing her short blond hair to stick straight up around her face. "She's making a killing with all these wet clothes from hikers."

It was here that I'd first met Queenie and Betts, along with Abby. I rolled into Normal in my broken-down RV to claim the luxurious Happy Trails Campground that was given to me by my then-criminal, now-dead ex-husband. Unfortunately, Happy Trails couldn't even be called livable at that time and looked nothing like the brochure my lawyer had given when he took the keys to my house in the Hamptons and my skyrise penthouse in Manhattan. Far from it.

I'd practically left New York City in the dumpy RV with the clothes on my back and a few things I'd picked up along the way at gas stations. When Dottie had told me how the campground laundry machines were broken down, she sent me here. Long story short, the Laundry Club ladies, which was what we were lovingly named by the community because we gathered here, and I had become fast friends.

We still came here to visit. After all, it had the luxuries of home with the couches and television sitting area, a coffee bar that was always stocked, a game station where there was always a puzzle to be finished, and a book club section where we had a monthly book club meeting.

Betts ran a tight ship, and that was why it was so successful.

"Okay. I just wanted to pop in and say hello when I saw you through the glass." I turned to leave.

"You aren't staying for the Winter Festival?" she asked.

"No." I lifted up the sleeve of my jacket and looked at my watch. "I'm working the office at the campground, and I've got to get going. I'm expecting new campers any minute now."

"Be careful," she called after me once I opened the door to leave. "It's getting slick out there."

I tugged the edges of my coat up around my neck to help shield me from the wind that'd suddenly picked up on my way to my car.

CHAPTER THREE

"Shhhh." *The darkness was all around me as the sound of a whisper curled in my ears. I was cradled in someone's arms. The faint smell of coal swept around me. "You're going to be just fine. Stay here and don't move."*

I yawned, wondering why my daddy was taking me outside and had placed me on the grass. I knew his smell from anywhere. He worked in the coal mine, and when he'd come home, Mama would make him hang his coat outside. Mama said it stunk, but I thought my daddy smelled good and looked so handsome.

A blast of flames brought me out of my sleep, and I jumped to my feet as the red, purple, and orange lights flickered from inside of my family home. The glass windows shattered and shot out like cannons. The fire lit up the sky, and I realized I was alone.

"Mama! Daddy!" I screamed into the dark. The hem of my long nightgown grazed my shins as the night breeze swept past me, chilling the tops of my feet.

Beep, beep, beep.

The sounds of the machine brought me back to the darkness and out of the nightmare of the house fire that I'd experienced as a child when all of my family died. All but me.

"Listen." The voice was unfamiliar to me as he talked in a hushed whisper. "The time is right now. Either you kill him, or I will."

Kill him? Kill who? Not that I could truly see what was going on, but I could hear. I dialed into my listening skills to make sure it wasn't coming from the TV.

"Maybe he will die. He's not even awake. Look around." There was a woman whispering now. "Everyone in here is practically on their deathbed. Why don't we see if he slips away peacefully?"

"He's done this a million times. Just do it. I don't care how you do. Smother him. Accidently trip over the machine to unplug the oxygen. Just do it." The man's voice was much harsher. "Or shoot him with this."

Don't do it. Do not kill anyone. I tried to open my mouth, but my lips wouldn't listen to me.

"What is that?" the woman asked.

"I don't know. Shoot it in that IV thing." The man was a little louder this time.

There was some shuffling, followed by footsteps.

"Hi," the familiar sound of the woman who had comforted Hank. But who was she?

"I thought you were doing a shift change." The woman who'd been whispering had a full voice. "Did you tell them how he's done this a few times before, and we aren't giving up hope?"

"I did. But I came back in because I thought I left something in here." Her footsteps were a little more frantic than before she'd greeted them. "Gosh. I guess I was wrong."

"What are you looking for?" the woman of the whispering duo asked.

"Nothing. You two get some rest. The emergency room can take it out of you. I know. I've been a nurse here for fifteen years this week." From the conversation, I was gathering that the woman who had been comforting Hank was a nurse, and I was in the emergency room. "He's lucky to have you, you know. I'll see you two tomorrow."

My heart began to race. There was some worry bubbling up in my head before a tingling began to tickle the tips of my fingernails. It was like a charge of lightning coursing through my veins. The realization that I, too, was in a coma or some sort of state that made me unable to communicate caused the early stages of an anxiety attack.

Even in this state, I wasn't able to control when these attacks happened. The back of my throat dried.

"You won't see us tomorrow." The man's voice shook me out of my own head. "Now, get this done."

"We better not get caught." The woman's voice cracked.

"Who's going to know? Visiting hours are over, with us being the one exception. And that girl next door is as dead as he is, only they are dragging out her death."

Wait. Was he referring to me?

"Hello." There was a different voice. "How's Mr. Lenz tonight?"

"No change. Do you think he'll come out of this?" The woman and man were stopped from smothering the poor patient.

"Rest assured that we are trying everything in our power to make sure he does." There was a little fiddling in the background that sounded like the nurse was clicking away on a keyboard and maybe checking his vitals. "His oxygen level is a little low, but with the ventilator, it'll help keep those levels up. I see by his chart that his kidney function is still good. I'll be back in to check on you."

There was a long pause. I strained to hear anything more, but the couple had gone eerily quiet.

Then came the sound that everyone knew because it was on all the hospital shows when someone died: the short beeps followed by a long and drawn-out beep that led to a flurry of activity before the zing of the curtains cut through.

"Randy? Randy?" the woman cried out. "Oh no. I think he. . ." her voice faltered.

There was a lot of chatter going on from various people I didn't recognize.

"Is he dead?" the man asked with a concerned tone.

"I'm sorry." There was a male's voice that apologized. "I'm afraid we couldn't save him this time."

The woman, who I recognized as one of the whisperers, cried out, "No. No. No!" followed by sobs.

"Now, now, honey. He's in a much better place now." The man was trying to comfort her.

"You're acting!" my voice escaped from my lips as my eyes flew open. "You murderer!" I flung up to sitting and gasped for breath.

The curtain zipped open between me and a few people I didn't recognize.

"Mae, you're awake." There was a man who was standing over what looked to be a dead man in a hospital bed. "Nurse, please go let Dr. Stricker know that Mae West has woken up."

"Her name is Mae West, as in the actress?" a woman standing next to the dead man asked with a tissue held to her face.

My heart raced. My mind was blank. What on earth was I doing in a hospital?

"Oh," I groaned when I lay back down. My entire body ached. "What happened?" I asked, resting my head against the pillow.

The nurse hurried over and closed the curtain between my bed and the dead guy's bed. But the horrified faces on the man and woman standing next to the dead guy didn't go unnoticed.

"You had a terrible car wreck, and you were brought in by ambulance." The nurse rushed around and began to check all of my vitals. "Do you remember what you were dreaming about when you woke up?"

"No." I tried not to talk too loudly. My head was having its own drum solo. "Was I dreaming?" I squinted.

"I bet you have a major concussion." She gave me a sympathetic look. "The doctor will give you something for your headache. But you sat straight up in bed and yelled 'murderer.'" She laughed and stuck the stethoscope on my chest. I shivered at the cold touch. "Maybe you were dreaming about your boyfriend. We practically had to shove him out the door when visiting hours were over. But I think he left his number with the last shift nurse, and she put it in your file. I'll call him."

"Good, because I have no idea what his phone number is without having my phone." I wondered where my phone was. "Isn't that terrible?"

"Honey, I have two children who have phones, and I couldn't tell you their phone numbers. All I do is scroll down and look for their names so I can hit the little send button." She peered down her nose at me and moved the stethoscope around. "I don't know why I bother. They never answer me anyways. These kids today, they don't do nothing but text."

The front of the curtain slightly opened. A man with gray streaks in his black hair popped his head in. Our eyes met. He pushed through the thin piece of cloth.

"I heard you were awake." He smiled. "I told everyone you were just having a nice concussion nap."

Concussion nap? Is that a thing? I wondered.

"Can you tell me your name?" he asked. "Full name."

"Maybelline Grant West," I managed to say through my dry mouth.

The nurse must've noticed and hurried over to the tray to fill up a Styrofoam cup with water from the plastic yellow pitcher. On her way back over, she stuck a sipping straw in it. She held it up to my mouth.

"Little sips at first," she instructed and let me take the cup. "Are you steady enough?"

I nodded, wanting to save what little energy I had to answer the doctor's questions.

He gave me a litany of questions that let him know I was aware of exactly who I was, my age, my birthday, and who the president was.

"What is your address?"

"I live at lot number 78 in Happy Trails Campground." I was so ready to go back to my little snuggly camper. My brows knotted. "I was supposed to go out to supper with Hank. I'd planned to have him stop by the nursery and pick me up a small tree for my camper."

"So you do live in a campground?" the doctor asked and looked at the nurse as if she knew.

"I do. I own it." I searched around but not without some pain. I grabbed my neck and winced.

"What are you looking for?" the nurse asked.

"My phone. I want to call my mom and boyfriend." I rubbed my neck.

"I told you that I'd let them know you're awake." The nurse gave a strange look to the doctor.

"Mae, are you having some pain?" the doctor asked.

I nodded.

"Can you tell me where?" He walked over, and when I pointed, he did some investigating. "I don't think you have anything broken. Just a banged-up head and some bruises, but we will do another scan just to make sure before I let you leave. You certainly have a concussion, which could last up to six or more weeks." He patted my hand in a fatherly figure kind of way. "You're going to have to take it easy. You're probably going to be dizzy with a little upset stomach, not wanting to eat a lot."

"Which is a shame because there's such good seasonal food. I love anything having to do with gingerbread." The nurse was a peppy little thing.

"I'm going to have you stay the rest of the night to keep an observation on you, but you can go home first thing in the morning." The doctor held my file to his chest and looked down at me. "I'll be sending you home with some pain meds, and I want you to take them. Hear me?"

"Yes, doctor." A long sigh escaped me, leaving me with some soreness in my chest.

"Your scan will tell us if you have any broken ribs. We were really concerned about your head." He pulled the file from his chest and opened it. He made a note or two then looked up at me. "Any questions before I go?"

"How long was I out?" I asked.

"About three hours." He patted my hand.

Three hours? Gosh, it felt like forever.

The curtain popped open, and another hospital employee walked in. He walked over and rested his hands on the handrail of the bed.

"Hey." He was jovial too. He even had on a pair of reindeer ears on a headband. "Can you tell me your name?" He picked up my hand and stared at my bracelet.

I told him.

"Date of birth?"

I told him that too.

"Looks like I've got the Mae West." He winked and moved around the bed, flipping the brakes off the wheels. "Wait until I go home and tell my wife that I took Mae West up for a scan. She loves all of your movies."

Yeah, yeah. There I went again, talking in my head. If I had a dime for every time someone made a movie joke about my name. . .Really, I was named after the cosmetic company, and I married a man with the last name West, but I just smiled.

"Don't you worry about a thing. You're in good hands with Preston. He'll have you back here in no time." The nurse tucked the bed covers up underneath me so they didn't hang. "While you're gone, I'll call your mama and your boyfriend."

Before I could tell her thank you, Preston had already rolled me out.

Preston was a talker. I wasn't paying attention to what he said. Instead, I was focusing on the flickering fluorescent lights in the ceiling tiles.

"Poor guy. I mean, he was knocking on death's door, but I sure didn't think it was today." He pushed a button on the wall, and the steel double doors opened. He pushed me in, and another male hospital employee walked over and took the file from the top of my legs.

"I'm the radiologist, and I'll be doing your scans." The young man smiled. "Are you claustrophobic?"

"No." I went to shake my head, but pain radiated down my back.

"Can I get your name?" He asked all the same questions and checked the ID bracelet around my wrist. "Mae West, huh?" He smiled. "You busy today?" he asked Preston and closed the file to give back to him.

"Yep. Can't stay. I'll be back. Had one die a little bit ago." Preston took the file and placed it in the plastic hanging file next to the door.

"Don't worry. I'll get him to the morgue and come right on up here to take you back."

I shivered.

"All right, Mae, let's get some pretty pictures of your insides." The radiologist pushed the bed next to a table. "Do you think you can slide on here?"

"Yes." I pushed with all my might, happy to see I had some strength left in me. Though it was a little painful, I worked through it.

I lay there while he entered a small room with a window and made sure I followed his instructions to a tee so I could get this right on the first try. I held my breath when he asked me to. I breathed when he asked me to. Soon enough, it was over.

Preston was back to get me, and when he rolled me back into the room, there were a couple of people inside who I didn't know.

"We just wanted to say that we are sorry you had to hear us about Randy," the man apologized.

"I'm sorry he didn't make it." I wasn't sure why they were apologizing to me when I should be giving them my condolences.

"We just hate that you had to," the woman spoke up before the man rudely interrupted her. She flipped her hair. The light caught her earring at just the right moment. It was sparkling so much that her face was blurred.

I had to look away when the shine made my head ache.

"We thought you were in a coma or something and are sorry you heard." The man seemed to be really agitated.

"I don't know if I was in a coma or just knocked out, but I didn't hear him die." I'd heard the death rattle could really throw people for a loop when their loved one was dying, and I was kind of glad I didn't hear him die because by the way they were acting, they seemed like I was in the room when he took his last breath.

"You didn't hear us telling him our final goodbyes?" the man asked.

I tried to blink away the spots from the lingering visual issues from those darn earrings. But there was no amount of blinking that made the black circle in the middle of his face go away.

"Oh no. I don't remember what happened to me, much less your. . ." I searched for the right words but came up empty because my curtain zipped open.

"Oh my gosh, Mae." Hank tore through that curtain and hurried to my side. "You came back to me." He ran his finger down my face, and past his outstretched arm, I noticed the couple had slipped behind the curtain where their loved one had died.

"You can't get rid of me that easy." I snickered.

"That's my baby girl. I see she's got her spunk back." Mary Elizabeth Moberly's voice was full of joy. "Give me some sugar." She practically pushed Hank out of the way and bent down to kiss me before she checked me out for herself.

"What did the doctor say?" she asked.

"He said I had a concussion and is sending me home in the morning." I stopped talking when I heard the nurse arguing on the opposite side of the curtain.

"I don't care if it's five o'clock in the evening or two o'clock in the morning. I'm going in there to see Maybelline Grant, and you can't stop me." Bobby Ray, my foster brother, sounded a little gruff. "This woman is going in with me whether you like it or not."

"There's certainly no smoking in here." The nurse was beside herself, but there was no way she was going to stop Bobby Ray and Dottie Swaggert from coming behind this curtain. "You have no respect for hospital rules," the nurse scoffed.

"Do you want me to show you what rule I live by?" Dottie Swaggert had had just about enough.

"Dottie!" I called.

Just then, the curtain swung open, and there stood Bobby Ray. Dottie was right behind him, cigarette dangling from the corner of her mouth.

CHAPTER FOUR

I'd love to say the doctor and nurse released me when Hank and all my friends as well as Mary Elizabeth came to spring me, but the doctor insisted he wanted to keep me for observation.

"How are you feeling this morning?" The morning-shift nurse had come in to introduce herself. "I'm Pamela, and I'll be here until the next shift change. If you need anything, let me know, even though I heard you're going home bright and early and probably before the day-shift nurses get here."

"You know, I'm rarely a negative person, but who on earth could get any sleep in here? They'd have to be someone hard of hearing." The noises from the emergency room had kept me up all night, which I was sure gave me more of a headache—nothing a good strong cup of coffee wouldn't fix. "Needless to say, I'm exhausted. I can't wait to be discharged."

"I know." She shook her head and smiled sweetly as she took my vitals then turned to the computer she'd rolled in. She grabbed her badge and flipped it over to scan the barcode to get into the computer and started typing. "You look great. Glad you only have a few bruises and nothing else. How's the head?"

"I'd like to think it's a headache due to no coffee." It didn't feel like the headache I'd had last night when I woke up.

"I can bring you a cup." She looked at the screen and used the mouse to hop around. "Dr. Mel has orders that he'll be in this morning to sign off on your release but no restrictions on food."

"Great." I pushed myself up a little and threw the scratchy sheet off me.

"What are you doing?" the nurse asked and hurried to my bedside.

"I was going to go grab myself a cup of coffee. I think the walk will do me some good."

"Let me help you stand. If you're steady on your feet, I think you'll be just fine to head on down the hall and get you a cup from the visitor's station if you want." She helped me get to my feet.

I was a bit woozy, but I was sure it was from not getting out of bed since they'd brought me in here. Plus, I was tired. I longed to be back in my cozy little camper with Fifi next to me, maybe Hank, with the television on some sappy Christmas movie and a cup of coffee along with the glow of a Christmas tree all lit up.

Only, I needed Hank to get me that tree. Or take me to get a tree like we were going to do before my car wreck.

"How do you feel?" she asked.

"Fine." I shrugged.

"Dizzy? Light-headed?" she asked.

"Nope. All good." I took a step, and I felt fine, so I took another one.

"Why don't I walk with you just in case." She wrapped her arm in the crook of mine. "I need a coffee too."

"Sure. I'd love the company." I grabbed the edge of the curtain and flung it back. The sound of the little metal balls on the curtain track made a zipping sound, and all the nurses at the nurses' station glanced up. "How long have you worked here, Pamela?"

"Just a couple of years. I'm pretty new compared to a lot of the nurses around here." She gestured the entire way around the emergency room, taking me to the coffee.

We must've been pretty close because I could smell it.

"Did you always want to work in the emergency room?" I asked, wondering why she'd picked here.

"I did. I had so many rounds during nursing school that I loved the business of the emergency room. Plus, you never know what is going to come in the door, so it really keeps me up on my nursing skills and knowledge." She pushed open a door that said Do Not Enter. "We can go into the nurses' room. Better coffee."

She entered what looked like a conference room. There were several dishes of food, doughnuts, and various baked items, along with a few big boxes of coffee from different coffee shops.

"Wow. Lots of choices." I laughed.

"Patients or their families send us a lot of food to thank us for caring for them or their loved ones." She sighed. "I'm going to go to the bathroom really quick, so pick what you want."

"Sure. Thanks." I walked over to the table and grabbed a small plate. My eyes had to be bigger than my stomach, because everything looked good, and I was piling it on.

"I dare you to undermine me again." The male voice came from the other side of the door.

The stern tone caught my attention, and I stood there, not daring to make a sound so I could hear. The doorknob to the room turned but returned back to its normal position like someone was going to come into the room but had decided not to.

"Who do you think you are, questioning my decisions? You're a nurse. I am a doctor."

The doctor sure wasn't happy with whoever he was talking to. I took a couple steps closer to the door and craned my ear up just to scratch my curiosity.

"You're the nurse. You take their temperature. Take them water. Do your job." He was brutal.

There was a little bit of sniffling coming from whoever he was talking to.

"What did you pick?" Pamela asked, causing me to jump and turn around. "Were you leaving with no food or coffee?" she questioned.

"I was just walking around," I lied, something I'd gotten good at doing since I'd kind of been nosing around crime scenes with the Laundry Club gals.

Technically, I was walking around. It wasn't a full lie, just a wee bit of one. There was no need to tell her I was slinking around so I could hear an argument between a doctor and a nurse.

The door opened, and a nurse walked in.

"Oh gosh!" She looked at me with a big, wide-open mouth. "You're awake." There was some delight across the blotted face of the nurse with the red-rimmed eyes. "You look scared."

"This is Raye Porter," Pamela introduced us. "She's the nurse who was on duty when you came in. She's a twelve-hour-shift nurse three days a week."

"You didn't hear." Raye's voice rose an octave. "I got the day-shift nurse manager position."

Pamela threw her hands over her mouth and bounced up and down on the balls of her feet before she ran over and threw her arms around Raye's neck.

"You deserve it. I'm so happy for you," Pamela squealed. "This is amazing news."

"Thank you." Raye's excitement had turned back to worry. She looked at me. "I'm so glad you're awake and up. Your boyfriend was so worried about you."

"Have I met you before?" I asked. "Have you come to Happy Trails Campground for any of the monthly get-togethers?" I asked.

"No." She shook her head.

"Your voice and name are familiar to me." I shrugged and picked one of the doughnuts off the plate, taking a big bite.

If they weren't staring at me, I would've spit it out. How on earth could they eat these? That was when I made a mental note, which in my state of concussion I hoped I'd remember, to send them some real doughnuts from the Cookie Crumble and coffee from Trails Coffee.

"Maybe you heard me while you were unconscious?" she suggested. "They say people do hear in an unconscious state."

"No. I don't remember hearing anything." I took a drink of the awful coffee in hopes it would help me wake up before the doctor came in and didn't decide to keep me. "I don't even remember the accident. I do remember talking to my friend, Queenie French, at the laundromat but nothing after that."

"All I know is you were brought in by ambulance when someone saw your car had gone off the road. When they brought you in, all of your vitals were good. You were just knocked out." She grabbed a cup and put it under the box-coffee nozzle, pouring herself some. "We were so happy you didn't have any brain swelling. Girl, someone above was watching out for you."

"Probably my family," I muttered with a hard swallow.

"I bet so." She didn't ask what I meant, even though I meant my entire family. "I swear my grandmother watches over me daily."

Pamela reached into the pocket of her scrubs and pulled out her phone. "I've got to run and clock out." Pamela put her hand on my arm. "My kiddos need me." She turned to Raye. "Do you think you could walk her back while I run and give a report so I can go home?"

"Sure." Raye seemed more than happy to continue our conversation.

"Good luck, Mae." Pamela put her hands together like she was praying for my speedy recovery. "And congratulations, Raye, on the new position. Much deserved."

I certainly wanted to know exactly what happened to me and after they brought me in.

"So did the EMTs say anything about my accident?" I asked as we made our way back down the hall, both of us with two big plates.

"They said if you didn't have your seat belt on, that you would've gone through the windshield and not survived." She looked at me through soft and sympathetic eyes. "I've seen so much in the last fifteen years. I've been here when tourists come and don't know our curvy roads. They drive way too fast and crash. Those are the ones who don't have on a seat belt and don't survive."

I gulped again at how serious my crash must've been.

"Do you know anything about my car?" I questioned.

"I think your boyfriend is a policeman, right?" We walked back into my emergency room cubicle.

"He's a detective," I corrected her.

"Oh. He mentioned something to one of your friends out in the lobby when I was giving an update to them, after you came in and before they could see you. I think he said your car was totaled." She helped me back into the bed and fluffed up the pillow behind my head. "I'm sorry."

"At least I'm alive." I lifted the coffee cup to my lips and eased back into the bed to wait for the doctor to come and give me my discharge paper, which wasn't too long after Raye left the room.

"I want you to take the pain medication as prescribed for the first couple of days at home." Doctor Mel handed me the paper prescription. "We are sending you home with a few, so you don't have to get it filled right away. I also want to make sure you rest when your body tells you to. The concussion you have can make you. . ." His voice faded off as I overheard someone just outside the curtain asking to see him.

My eyes shifted between Dr. Mel's moving lips and the sets of feet I could see underneath the curtain.

"Dr. Mel." Raye had pushed back the curtain slightly. "Randy Lenz's family is here to see you."

"I'll be with them in a second, Raye." He held up a finger with the biggest attitude like he didn't like her interrupting.

"If you need to go talk to them, I'll be fine." I wanted to let him know it was okay with me. "I can get dressed while you talk to them." Then I realized I didn't have any clothes but the ones they'd literally cut off me to put on the less-than-flattering hospital gown.

"I'll just be a second." He took me up on my offer.

Since there weren't any clothes to put on, and all I could do was wait for Hank to show up, I couldn't help but eavesdrop on the heated conversation going on between Dr. Mel and the Randy Lenz family, whoever they were.

"I'm telling you, I want an autopsy of my father," someone demanded.

"But the paperwork was signed off on last night." Raye's voice was definitely a voice I'd heard from somewhere, but where?

"Oh." I groaned and rubbed my head when I tried to recall where I'd heard her voice because my head hurt.

"I am the next of kin, and no one gave you permission to get any other signatures. I demand to see the paperwork," Randy Lenz's family member said. "Or I'll call the family lawyer."

"I'm sure we can get this all straightened out without lawyers involved." The good old doc was trying to reason with the family member.

"I want an autopsy or else."

My head moved side to side to get a good glimpse underneath the curtain as one set of feet walked away.

"I told you this was going to get ugly," Doctor Mel said before he pulled the curtain back open with a big smile on his face, nurse Raye standing next to him.

Her face was flushed with a shocked look in her eyes. Or maybe it was a faraway look, as if she were remembering something. It was an expression that actually haunted me.

"Now, let's get you out of here." Dr. Mel came in and grabbed my chart. He flipped it open. It was amazing how he could turn off any emotion he had from his conversation under a minute ago. "I want to see you back here in two days to check on your concussion. My office is located in the doctors' building next door."

"Sounds good." I sat on the edge of the bed and continued to listen to the instructions before my heart leapt out of my chest when Hank Sharp walked in.

CHAPTER FIVE

"No joke. Did you hear that nurse give me some flap-jaw?" Dottie still wasn't letting go of the nurse not wanting to let her in, and two days had gone by.

"Drop it, Dottie." Queenie French was trying her hardest to do some sort of stretch in the tiny hallway of my RV. "It's over. Look at the bright side of things."

"I am. I'm looking at how to handle her, and you want to give them some treats from the Cookie Crumble." Dottie rolled her eyes.

"I wanted to go down to the Winter Festival and see the booths before it ends this week. Plus, I can't wait to try Christine Watson's final version of her eggnog." I looked at my phone and noticed it was almost time for Hank to get off work and come get me.

The day had already flown by, and sitting here was driving me nuts. I peered up at the clock on the camper wall. It was a fancy digital with the temperature and date on it. I mainly used it for the temperature, to help me decide how I needed to dress for the day. There were two things it told me as of now: one, it was too cold to muster up the effort to get all bundled up to go for a walk so that I wasn't cooped up in the camper, and two, I still had about an hour until Hank got off work, which was seven o'clock. By the time we got down to the festival, we might just make it to see one of the shows the Normal Baptist Church was putting on.

"It's deee-vine. I mean, hands down the best eggnog I've ever tasted. And I've had a lot of eggnog." Mary Elizabeth hadn't left my side since I'd gotten home. She fiddled with her pearls around her neck.

She wanted me to go stay at The Milkery, the bed-and-breakfast she owned with Dawn Gentry, but I knew her rooms were booked. Just like every other business in the Daniel Boone National Park, we did everything we could to have customers during the winter months. The Milkery was no different. So taking up a room that she could keep renting was not a good decision for me to make.

Besides, I loved my camper. It was my home on wheels.

"Well, I reckon I better get back up to the office." Dottie snapped open the top of her cigarette case and tapped it on the side of her finger until the butt of a cigarette jumped out. She lifted the case up to her lips and stuck the end of the cigarette in her mouth. "You need anything before I go?"

My phone rang. "Nope. It's Hank. I bet he's on his way." I couldn't answer his call fast enough.

Mary Elizabeth and Queenie walked out of the camper with Dottie, which was unusual, especially with all the snow on the ground. I could only conclude they were out there talking about me.

With one ear pressed to the phone and the other trying to hear what Mary Elizabeth was saying to Dottie and Queenie, everyone's words started to mix up in my head.

"What? Did you just say you're not coming home?" I questioned Hank when his words finally pressed through the noise and pain in my head. "I swear I thought you said something about a suspicious death."

"Mae, it's too much for you. I'm sorry." Hank's voice dropped. "I know you've got a concussion, and I'm not being very good at remembering that when I talk to you because I only want you to be all better."

There was a hint of fear in his voice, but I didn't have time to assure him I was fine. I wanted to know about this suspicious death. That would definitely take my mind off the concussion.

"No. I'm fine. You're fine. Mary Elizabeth is here with Queenie. They are outside talking to Dottie, and I was trying to eavesdrop when you called. That's all," I assured him. "What is this about a suspicious death?"

"Not that you need to worry about it, but last night, there was a man in the emergency room next to you. He was in really bad shape, and from what I can gather, he'd been sick for a while." The sound of shuffling papers came from Hank's end of the phone. "According to the hospital reports, he's been in and out of the hospital the last six months. His family had ordered an autopsy, and it came back there was an overdose of potassium in his bloodstream."

It struck me this was the guy the family members were talking about with Doctor Mel, who I'd overheard on the other side of the curtain.

"Hank," I gasped. "I over—" I was about to tell him how I overheard Dr. Mel and the nurse fussing this morning when I'd gone to get coffee with my nurse, Pamela, but I couldn't recall the other nurse's name.

Concussion. I blamed my lack of recall on the concussion.

"Mae, listen," he rudely interrupted, "I have to go take another call. Please go let Chester out." Then he hung up.

"Did you literally just hang up on me before I could say goodbye?" I asked out loud, which only made the voice in my head tell me there was something big happening here.

I stroked Fifi's back as I tried desperately to remember exactly what I'd overheard. Using my memory was proving to be a difficult task while having a concussion.

I picked Fifi up and decided to grab the notebook the Laundry Club ladies and I'd used in the past to help solve a few mysteries that had plagued our little town. Though none of us were qualified to solve crimes, we declared in our right and with the track record of solving a few that our super nosey skills of sniffing things out did come in handy.

Some of those clues we'd picked up did offer Hank or even Sheriff Jerry Truman some great information that helped solve burglaries and even murders.

Which brought me back to the notebook. I got the notebook from the junk drawer in my galley kitchen and took out a pen. The rambles of Mary Elizabeth's voice went in one ear and out the other as Fifi and I nestled back on the couch.

"Let's see if we can remember anything." I talked to Fifi like she understood me, and by her licking my chin, it was good enough confirmation for me. I pulled the blanket up around us and clicked the pen. "Hank said a family member wanted the autopsy, but I didn't recognize the voice. So it means another family member had come forward."

Though it was a wee bit foggy, I did remember those two people who had apologized to me when Hank had come in to see me the first time. I'd have to jog his memory, though I'm sure he remembered a lot more than me right now. I couldn't recall their exact wording or who they said they were.

"I'm not sure they did tell me their names." I wrote down how they'd apologized to me about their loved one dying, though they didn't seem as concerned as the voice I'd heard later in the morning who had insisted. . .

I clapped my hands when I remembered what she'd said.

"I'm telling you, I want an autopsy of my father," someone demanded.

"But the paperwork was signed off on last night."

I still believed I'd heard Raye's voice before, but it hurt my head to try and recall. Instead, I found I had to really focus on what was in front of me, and that was writing down the exact conversation I'd overheard.

"I am the next of kin, and no one gave you permission to get any other signatures. I demand to see the paperwork," Randy Lenz's family member said. *"Or I'll call the family lawyer."*

"I'm sure we can get this all straightened out without lawyers involved."

When I remembered Dr. Mel saying those words, I recalled a very concerned tone in his voice that clearly told me there was something he didn't want the Lenz family to know.

"I want an autopsy or else." Randy Lenz's daughter didn't seem like she was buying any of Dr. Mel's words.

"I told you this was going to get ugly." Those words from Dr. Mel sent a

chill through my bones, and I knew Dr. Mel was covering something up.

But what?

The only way I knew how to find out who all the people in this family triangle were was to take those cookies to the nurses like I'd already planned.

CHAPTER SIX

"Let's go." I flung my purse with the notebook inside over my shoulder and headed straight over to Mary Elizabeth's car with a determined giddyup in my step because I knew she was going to give me some grief.

"It's almost pitch-dark outside. Where on earth are we going? And you do not need to be driving," Mary Elizabeth insisted after I walked outside, where she, Dottie, and Queenie stood with pinched lips, a sure sign they were talking about me or at least something they didn't want me to hear.

"The doctor said to give you a few days of rest, and driving isn't resting your brain." Mary Elizabeth stepped in front of the driver's-side door.

"Dottie, please go let Chester out and check on Fifi a couple of times," I said to her over my shoulder and proceeded to open the car door. "That's why I'm having you drive me—because I don't have a car."

"Oh, right." Mary Elizabeth gnawed on her cheek. "Why don't we call Hank and let him know what you're doing?"

"Do you even know where I'm going?" I asked because I'd yet to tell her.

"Well. No." Her eyes snapped up to mine. "And at seven o'clock?"

"I want you to take me to the Cookie Crumble so I can grab some doughnuts for the nice nurses who took care of me since I went in late afternoon and overnight." I knew that a polite gesture would be something Mary Elizabeth would be all over.

"Why didn't you say so in the first place?" She wiggled her shoulders and straightened up. "I'm so glad some of the manners you learned in that awfully expensive etiquette class have stuck with you all of these years."

"La-di-da." Dottie rolled her eyes and took a long drag of her cigarette. "Did you hear that, Queenie? Etiquette class," she said sarcastically.

"I've got to get going. I'm teaching a public Jazzercise class at the amphitheater for the Winter Festival before Betts and her choir take the stage." Queenie plunged forward into a runner's lunge. "It's an amazing dance mix and flex class so these hikers don't get a charley horse when they are hiking to the cascades." Queenie lifted up and turned to me. "Honestly, you should come do some stretches. Jazzercise helps with the right brain and left brain as you watch the moves and try to do them. And you can grab some doughnuts from Christine's booth."

"She has a booth?" I asked and couldn't help but notice the looks on their faces. "Oh gosh, I remember." Clearly my memory wasn't as sharp as it was before the accident, but at least I remembered. "She's got the drink of the festival." I snapped my fingers, looking up as I tried to recall, which took me a second. "Eggnog! Christine Watson's eggnog is the festival's drink."

"I think you need some more rest." Mary Elizabeth's brows pinched. "I can't take it if I let you go out and something worse happens."

"We are going to the hospital." I snickered, playing off the lack of memory and how slow I was to recall information. "What better place to be if something happens?" I shrugged and got into the car.

The three of them shared glances with each other and nodded in agreement before they said their goodbyes, mumbling something under their breaths that they didn't want me to hear before Mary Elizabeth got back into the car.

"You have no idea how delighted I am that you're going to be okay." She still sounded worried.

"Going to be?" I needed to put her mind at ease. "I am okay. It's just going to take a little bit of time before my concussion goes away. Taking the doughnuts to the nurses is a nice etiquette I learned way back when." I hid the real reason I was going to the hospital, but she didn't need to know that.

The snowflakes were softly falling to the ground, instantly melting once they hit the pavement, or it at least looked as such. There was a known condition on these curvy roads during the winter months that meteorologists loved to refer to as black ice.

"Black ice." I groaned and stared out the window just as the memory of me driving to the campground right before my accident flashed before me. "I think I hit black ice."

"That's what Jerry said he believed happened too." Mary Elizabeth gripped the wheel. "That's why I'm driving slowly. I've got precious cargo in this car." She looked over and smiled.

"I'm sorry about all of this." I stared out the window and tried to recall exactly what had happened. "Where is it that I wrecked?"

The road we were on was the only road from Happy Trails Campground to downtown Normal, where I'd left the Laundry Club before my car wreck.

"You don't need to be bothered with that." She pooh-poohed. "You just need to heal."

"Good ole southern mom you are." I couldn't help myself. "Sweeping everything under the rug. Everything."

"I'm not telling you to sweep it under the rug." Her tone took a hard turn. "You need to let yourself heal."

"How long will it take me to heal from the death of my family?" I had no idea where that came from, but some part of my subconscious had taken over. Immediately, I slapped my hand over my mouth.

"Maybelline Grant." Mary Elizabeth gasped. "What on earth are you talking about? I've always encouraged you to talk about your family and your feelings."

"It didn't seem like that a couple of months ago when you had me go do that therapy with naked Tex." I shook my head and knew I'd just opened a can of worms.

Tex was a chiropractor who lived in a hippie camp near the cascades. He had adjusted Mary Elizabeth's back to full health and strength. When she wrangled me on the trail to see him, telling me I needed this Reiki-type therapy to deal with my past, I'd had some memories that needed to be explored.

"You told me you needed to explore your past. I never held you up." She slowly veered the car off to the side of the road and put her emergency flashers on before she popped the gearshift into park. "You have to be the one to take the first step. I'm here to hold your hand and wipe the tears while you do it."

I gulped. "I'm sorry. You're right," I apologized. "I'm sorry I upset you and made you pull over."

"You didn't make me pull over." She peeled her hands off the steering wheel and pointed past my nose.

I stared out the window and saw the trunk of a tree with all the bark peeled off of it.

"Is that what I hit?" I asked, even though I knew it in my gut.

Before she could confirm it, I jumped out of the car, causing my purse to fall to the floorboard, where practically everything spilled out. My feet nearly slipped out from underneath me, and I grabbed the door handle and looked down.

Black ice.

"You said you wanted to see, and against my better judgment, I stopped only because you accused me of not letting you remember your past." Mary Elizabeth had gotten out and walked to meet me on the passenger side.

"Be careful," I cautioned so she wouldn't fall and break a hip. I reached out my hand for her to grasp for support as she rounded the bumper.

"I never wanted you to not remember your past." She squeezed my hand. "I didn't want you to feel pain. I want you to know you are loved no matter what happened to you."

"I know. I'm sorry. It's my concussion." I shrugged.

"No. I'd love to think that." She smiled, not letting me off the hook. "But you've always been a little spitfire and a little mouthy. That concussion has nothing to do with how you feel right now or any other time. Good excuse though."

She stepped toward the tree, taking my hand along with her as she forced my feet to take the first step.

"I got the call from Hank that you were taken to the hospital in an ambulance. He said the EMTs said you were stable with no bleeding but a few bruises." Her eyes scrutinized my forehead, at the big goose egg that'd formed overnight. "It was the worst call I'd ever gotten." She let go of my hand once she appeared to be on solid footing. She placed it on the trunk of the tree. "I'm so blessed your life wasn't taken and this tree sacrificed itself for you."

"What?" I laughed, thinking Mary Elizabeth had lost her marbles.

Slowly she peeled back a part of a low hanging branch and nodded beyond it to a cliff just a few feet from the tree.

"If your car would've gone just one inch to the right, you'd gone over the cliff, and I'm not sure we'd ever find you. . ."

I didn't let her finish up her train of thought. I curled her into my arms as she let out sobs of relief, releasing what could've happened.

"I'm okay. I'm fine," I assured her but was unable to look past her head to the edge where it was all too real just how dangerous the Daniel Boone National Park was if you weren't experienced and careful. These types of cliffs were all over the forest.

"I'm sorry," I kept whispering to her, feeling so grateful for the tree. It was a solid fact. The tree was there to save me. I didn't die. I was spared.

Then my brain kicked in, like cobwebs being dragged away from a corner by a broom. I was meant to hear Randy Lenz's death. I was still here, and I had an obligation to solve his murder. At least I think he was murdered. But why did I think that?

There was a gut feeling that I knew more than I could remember.

"Now that we've given the tree some love, why don't we just put this behind us and go get those doughnuts so we can give some gratitude to the nurses at the hospital who took really good care of me?"

So I had a motive. So what?

"Are you sure you feel up to it? You just got out." The worry lines on her forehead deepened.

"I think the time is now." I smiled, putting her hand in the bend of my arm for her to hold on to as we made our way through the lightly fallen layer of snow in the grass between us and the car. "I also think we can just stop at the festival and get them."

She tapped my hand before grasping her other one that was tucked around my elbow. "Oh, Mae." She sighed. "I know you so well. Don't think I didn't see the notebook tumble out of your bag when you got out of the car. You might as well tell me what's going on up in that concussed mind of yours."

"Get in the car." I was caught, which was better anyways. I could be the brains behind the operation while she could do a little more snooping for me.

CHAPTER SEVEN

I gave Mary Elizabeth the rundown on our way downtown.

"When Hank told me about the guy next to me dying and his autopsy came back suspicious, I remembered a conversation with one of Randy's family members," I told her.

"Who is Randy?" she asked and pulled her car into the Laundry Club parking lot.

"He was the dead guy next to me." I wasn't sure if she was playing a game with me to see if my concussion had made me delusional or if she really wasn't following along. "He's the guy Hank said died of potassium, only he wasn't on potassium, which means someone gave him liquid potassium."

"I thought potassium was good for you." Mary Elizabeth turned the car off.

"The Winter Festival looks like a hit." I was pleasantly surprised at the foot traffic on both sides of Main Street. "And look," I gushed and pointed across the street where Gert Hobson had set up an old-time coffee stand with vintage coffee cups hanging from the trees in the side yard of Trails Coffee Shop.

There were several freestanding heaters that dotted the side yard, with picnic tables instead of her usual café tables. She had some carolers dressed in vintage clothing. The women had on bonnets, and the men were in top hats.

"Your idea really was great." Mary Elizabeth snuggled up with me, putting her gloved hands in the bend of my arm. "You will be just fine once your concussion goes away."

"I already feel fine. It's honestly a bump on the head." I played it off even though I had a smidgen of a headache. I refused to take any of the pain medication Dr. Mel had prescribed. I didn't like the way the medication made me woozy if I didn't need it. Right now, my headache wasn't too bad.

"Oh, look." I had caught Betts Hager's eye when we walked past the Laundry Club. She waved me in. "Let's go in for a minute."

"But I thought you wanted to get doughnuts, take them to the hospital, and then go home to bed where you belong." Mary Elizabeth tried to lay the mothering on me, but I kept going.

"Look at you." Betts hurried over after I swung the door open. "You look great."

"You are a true friend." I cackled and pulled my hair back from my forehead so she could see the big goose egg. "And these aren't from lack of sleep."

There wasn't any amount of makeup that was going to cover up the double-bruised eyes.

"You're beautiful inside and out." She grabbed both my hands. "And alive. That's all that matters."

"You said hello." Mary Elizabeth grabbed the sleeve of my coat. "Let's go get those doughnuts. The faster we go, the quicker we get you back in bed so you can nurse those bumps and bruises."

I eased down onto the couch, which was right next to the door.

"Are you okay?" Mary Elizabeth crouched next to me.

"Do you mind going to get the doughnuts for me?" I rubbed my hands along the thighs of my jeans. "I'll just wait right here."

"Let me get you a water." Betts took off toward her office where she had her own stash of snacks instead of using the vending machines, which she kept stocked for the laundromat customers. She offered free coffee but not free snacks.

"Of course I will." Mary Elizabeth's voice cracked.

"I'm fine. You know, just resting." I couldn't dare stand to see her so worried, but I had to get her out of here so I could be alone with Betts and fill her in on what was happening. "Here. Take my wallet."

She refused. I opened it and took a few bills out, stuffing them in her coat pocket.

"You're making my head hurt worse," I told her so she'd stop harassing me about paying for the doughnuts.

*Maybe this headache gig isn't a bad excuse to use . . .*I started. How on earth could I think this way? I shoved the little evil side to the back of my head. I was relieved when Mary Elizabeth gave in and left to go buy the doughnuts.

"Here you go." Betts came back with a bottle of water.

"No thanks. I'm good." I pushed it away and reached in my purse for the notebook. "Listen, we've got a murder to solve."

"Murder?" Betts's big brown eyes grew to the size of half-dollars. "What's your name?"

"May-bell-ine Grant West." I drew out my name for silliness's sake. "I sent Mary Elizabeth away so I could tell you what we are going to be doing."

"We? Oh no." Betts wagged her finger at me, shook her head, and took a few steps backwards. "You aren't using some sort of head concussion to bring me into your shenanigans."

"Betts." I gasped like I was offended that she had accused me of such things. "I never."

"You never?" She laughed. "You have ever, and every single time we try to solve one of these crazy crimes, we end up being at the butt end of the bad guy."

"This time, we don't have to do that because it took place at the hospital." I opened the notebook.

"You've already started to write things down?" she asked.

The bell over the door dinged. Both of us looked.

"What did I just walk into?" Abby Fawn's gaze shifted back and forth.

"Mae is just fine. She can't possibly have a concussion." Betts twisted open the water and took a big swig.

"I just saw Mary Elizabeth, and she told me you were feeling ill, so I came over right away." Abby eased down next to me. Her eyes darted between the notebook and my face. "Are you pretending? Why do you have our sleuthing notebook out?" There was an uptick in her voice. She bounced with excitement, her ponytail flinging side to side. "Gimme." She reached out for the notebook.

"I knew you'd be excited." I dug into my purse to get a pen. "Here."

"You two are killing me. Why on earth are we doing this?" Betts continued to ask questions while Abby read over the notes.

We ignored Betts. Both of us knew she would be the first one to drive us in her big cleaning van to find clues.

"Wait. There were two people who came over from the dead man's side of the curtain and apologized for what you heard?" Abby wanted clarification.

"Yeah. But I didn't hear the man die. I was out." I shrugged. "But that's not the weird part." I seriously had to remember to ask Hank about the two people who were standing there when he came in to see me.

"This morning, when Dr. Mel was discharging me, a family member of Randy Lenz insisted on an autopsy. Dr. Mel said someone had signed off that they didn't want an autopsy."

"So why does this make it a homicide?" Betts finally started to come around.

"You know lawyers. They get their noses stuck in everything. According to Randy's daughter, she was going to get her lawyer if they didn't do an autopsy. Well, Hank canceled on me because the initial autopsy report came back that Randy had been injected with an overdose of potassium when he wasn't even supposed to get potassium."

"I'm out." Betts put her hands up in the air. "If Hank is already on the case, then we just need to enjoy our Christmas. Especially now that you almost died."

"I didn't almost die." I rolled my eyes at how overly dramatic Betts was acting. "We don't have a lot of time before Mary Elizabeth gets back." I motioned for Abby to keep going.

Abby's shifty eyes told me she didn't know whether she should continue or not.

"It's not like we are going to go deep undercover or anything. It's just to help me take my mind off the wreck and concussion." I started to play the sick card.

"Don't you dare, Mae West." Betts lifted the bottle back up to her lips to drink. Her eyes held mine. "We know you. We know how you operate."

"And it's always been out of the goodness of my heart." I could tell by the looks on their faces that they weren't going to bite. They were right. I didn't have a real reason for us to go behind Hank's back and try to figure out who was murdered in the room next to me and why.

"But they apologized for me hearing something." My eyes lowered, and I kept talking to myself even though they were pretending not to listen. "What did I overhear? Or what did those people think I over-heard? Did they kill him?"

"Do you remember us talking to you when you were unconscious?" Abby was reeled back in.

"Abby, don't fall for it." Betts shook her head and walked over to a counter in the laundromat where she offered a service in which customers could drop off their laundry for her to do instead of them doing it. "She's baiting us." Betts picked up a bedsheet and neatly folded it.

"They say people can hear when they are unconscious, so maybe they were talking or killed him and you heard it." Abby's eyes grew. She sat down on the couch with her hands folded between her knees. "Do you think you heard the murder?" she asked, leaning in a little closer.

"I don't remember anything. All I remember is. . ." my voice trailed off. My jaw dropped. "I think I sat up in bed and yelled 'murderer' when I woke up."

"You did what?" Betts groaned. "Oh no. No." She shook her head. "Hank was a mess when you weren't awake and lying in that bed. He would die if he knew you were doing this right now."

I gave her a flat look. My stomach sank when I heard the bell ding, knowing it was Mary Elizabeth.

"There you are."

I was never so glad in my life to see that it was Ava Cox. Her eyes focused on me.

"I just saw Mary Elizabeth in that long line at the Cookie Crumble booth. She told me you had a horrible crash and were in the emergency room." Ava peeled off her knit cap. Strands of her long black curls lifted into the air from static electricity.

"I'm fine," I assured her. "I don't need a lawyer. Maybe the tree I hit does," I teased.

Ava Cox and I had a rocky history. She'd been a victim in more ways than one when I was with my now-dead ex-husband and his Ponzi scheme. Since then, our paths crossed a few times, and by 'crossed,' I mean all of them had to do with a crime. All of them from me sticking my nose into them, just like I was doing now.

"I wasn't thinking you did." Ava glanced around at me, Abby, and Betts. "That's why I'm here. If you were in the emergency room last night, I want to know if you remember seeing or hearing anything about one of my new clients' father. He was murdered in the emergency room last night."

"Randy Lenz?" Abby questioned and nudged me.

"Yes. How did you know?" Ava asked.

"Mae is already snooping." Betts took a vested interested now that Ava had come into the picture.

Ava Cox was a lawyer. She'd recently moved to Normal and had asked us to help her on a case, which we did, and we solved it. It was one of those instances Betts had referred to where we'd put ourselves at the end of the killer's weapon.

In the end, it all turned out fine. We were no worse for the wear.

"Good. My client is Denise Lentz. She insists someone killed her father. When the autopsy report came back that he had been overdosed with potassium, we knew it was murder. What did you hear?"

"I'm not sure I heard anyone getting murdered." It was a good time to circle back to a few questions I had. "Why would anyone want to murder him?" I needed that piece of the puzzle before we all made a deal with Ava to snoop around. After all, that was why she was here.

When she moved to Normal, she made it very clear that it would be worth our while if we helped her with some of her clients and to find some answers when she needed them. Most of the situations so far, outside of one murder, were things like gossip: who was cheating with who, who was sticking money in their pockets from their business illegally. Just minor things. But murder. . .that got my blood pumping.

"Mr. Lenz was at his work's holiday party when he fell ill. It was there that he was going to announce to his employees he was retiring, and his daughter, Denise, was going to step into his shoes." Ava scrutinized each one of us like she was in front of a jury.

Out of the corner of my eye, I could see Abby was already making notes in the notebook.

"It seems awfully suspicious he got sick at the party. Then they took him to the emergency room, where he was expected to come home but didn't." Ava's eyes clouded with suspicion.

"If you think it's someone in the company, then who? Who thought they would be next in line before Denise?" Betts asked and walked over to the coffee stand, where she retrieved a few mugs and the carafe.

"He has been dating a woman by the name of Georgia Gammon. They met when she started working for the company five years ago. Not only did she worm her way up to senior vice president but also became his companion." Ava made it sound as if Randy's death was caused by a scorned-woman motive.

"You think she wanted the position when he retired, so she killed him?" Abby stopped writing to get a coffee from Betts as Betts dolled them out to us.

"I think she has a great motive. She is eighteen years younger than him. She and Denise do not get along. And he'd yet to sign an agreement to have Denise take over. According to Denise, he was going to sign the papers that night as a Christmas gift to her." The steam off the coffee mug Ava had brought to her lips curled up around her nose.

"How do you know he didn't decide to change his mind and told Denise that before the party, so she was the one who killed him?" It was the shoe-on-the-other-foot scenario.

"Could be." Ava sighed. "But I'm hired by Denise, who insisted on the autopsy. Don't you think she'd have just left well enough alone if she did it?"

"Not if he had the company going to someone else." Abby's eyes shifted between me and Ava. "What if he did decide not to give it to Denise, and say he chose to leave it to this Georgia lady. Denise got mad. Denise killed her father, and what a great way to shift the blame to Georgia, unless there was a witness to the documents for the turnover of the company."

"That's why I need you to snoop for me while I file all the paperwork to get the documents from the hospital and the sheriff's department." Gingerly, Ava set the coffee cup on the table before she stood up. "We need to get into the company and see what employees know what, go see the nurses to figure out who it was that signed off on his death certificate, and determine if anyone saw or heard anything."

"I didn't hear a thing, but there was a lady and a man that opened the curtain between me and Randy's emergency room where they apologized to me." I really wished I could remember. "I had no idea what they were apologizing for, but it was something. When Hank came into the room, they left, so maybe he can remember what they were saying. The last thing I did hear was someone who claimed to be Randy Lenz's daughter telling Dr. Mel that she insisted on an autopsy, that she wasn't there when he died. She also demanded to know who was there."

"She has to the right to know." Ava clearly believed in her client, but I'd been around this block a time or two when the most obvious killer was generally closest to the victim.

"How much do you plan on giving us?" I got down to the nitty-gritty. She didn't need to know that I was already planning on sticking my nose into the already messy situation, and if the Laundry Club gals and I could benefit in the monetary way, especially during the winter months when tourism was down, then I was all for it.

After a little back-and-forth, we finally settled on a number that benefited all of us, even Dottie, since she wasn't present.

"I'll keep you posted on anything Denise has to contribute." Ava tugged on her gloves.

"We'll be in touch." I got up and walked her to the door. "Mary Elizabeth." I greeted my foster mom.

She was coming in as Ava was going out. They greeted each other with southern pleasantries before Ava went on her way.

"Are you ready to take the doughnuts to the hospital nurses?" I asked Mary Elizabeth with the alternate motive firmly planted in my head.

"Look at the time." Betts scurried off into her office, quickly emerging with her heavy coat in her hands. "The choir has a performance, and based on the earlier appearance, we are going to need to practice at the church tomorrow. I hope they sound better tonight."

CHAPTER EIGHT

The hospital was actually about thirty minutes west of Normal. Though it was still considered part of the Daniel Boone National Forest, it wasn't in the park or in Normal.

There were so many questions running through my head that Ava hadn't addressed. Things like Randy Lenz's company name, where it was located, and other details like that.

Ava wanted us to get in front of some of his employees, which we could use Betts's cleaning service to do or even possibly get Queenie to do a free Jazzercise demonstration for employees.

Employee health and wellness had been a big thing in companies lately, so this could possibly be the angle we could use. No doubt Queenie would be up for it. I quickly texted Ava my questions while Mary Elizabeth drove us to the hospital.

"You aren't listening to a thing I've said." Mary Elizabeth huffed. "Are you sure you don't want to get checked out while we are here?"

I looked up as she maneuvered her car into the hospital parking lot.

"Gosh. That was fast." I put my phone in my purse. "I'm sorry if you didn't feel like I was listening. I was just lost in my thoughts."

Though Mary Elizabeth was a good confidant, and I still considered her my mom even though she didn't birth me, which meant she was going to worry about me. Other times, I was totally open to sharing about my sleuthing—to her protest, but she usually got in on the action. This time, I figured it was too close to home and she'd deter me from it. Especially if this concussion was present.

"Anything you want to share?" she asked.

"I am wondering how I can tap into those subconscious memories of when Hank, you, and the girls were by my bedside. I really do think there's something to this. I'd love to remember all of y'all talking to me." I smiled and sighed. "I'm sure it's what got me through." I didn't lie to her. I did want to know what I could've possibly heard. I wanted to know what those two people had apologized to me for and what they thought I'd heard.

"You can always go see Texas." Mary Elizabeth brought up her bare-chested hippie chiropractor who we'd discovered in the fall while hiking.

I snorted.

"What?" She asked. "Did you forget he unlocked some of your memories you buried about your family's fire?"

"I wasn't laughing at that. I was thinking about Tex and this weather. Where are they now?" Tex and his hippie commune lived in the woods.

"They built a yurt." Mary Elizabeth shocked me with how much she knew. "What is that look for? He has helped me tremendously with my hips, so I still go see him twice a month."

"I had no idea, but sure, I'd be open to see what he can unlock." I was game. "You're right. He did unlock some of my past."

"And you've yet to really explore it." Mary Elizabeth turned the car off, letting her statement linger as we got out.

"It's not that I haven't explored it. I haven't had time to explore it." Tex had opened a memory that I hadn't allowed myself to explore too much. "Happy Trails was hopping busy, and now we have the holidays. Maybe I'll have time to dig deeper during the winter months."

The winter months were technically January and February. Those were the really lean months and made it hard for campers to come and stay at the campground. It was not economical for me as a businessperson to keep all the campers open for rent or the bungalows.

The water lines in a camper had to be properly insulated during the winter months so they wouldn't burst and ruin the camper. Henry winterized a few of the campers, and a couple were properly insulated. The bungalows didn't have HVAC, heating and air-conditioning units, so we didn't keep those open either.

Bobby Ray, my foster brother, lived in one of the bungalows, and he'd installed a pellet stove to keep his home nice and warm.

Speaking of Bobby Ray, I needed to see him about a new car. Not really a new car, a new-to-me car.

"See." Mary Elizabeth popped the door handle. "There you go again, getting lost in your head."

I laughed and got out. "Actually, I wasn't lost. I was thinking about Bobby Ray and how I need a new car." I met her on the driver's side and opened the back-seat door to grab the box of doughnuts.

"I can drive you around for now." Mary Elizabeth gave me a hard stare. "When Dr. Mel gives you the clear to drive, then we can talk about getting you a new car. In the meantime, I love spending time with you."

"Let's go." I was blessed to have found a foster mother who really did love me and Bobby Ray. There were so many people in the system like me, only they didn't get a good placement like I'd gotten.

"Which reminds me." Mary Elizabeth dug into her purse as we walked to the sliding doors of the hospital. "My mail is still being forwarded from Perrysburg to The Milkery. This came for you."

I opened the envelope once we made it through the doors and quickly scanned the letter.

"A reunion of the foster kids I was placed with. Like a class reunion." There was no way I was going to this.

"When is it?" Mary Elizabeth asked.

"In the spring." I resisted from ripping it to shreds and put it in my purse.

"Mae," a glee-filled voice said. "I didn't expect to see you back so soon. Are you okay?" A woman in a nurse's uniform hurried from behind the admissions counter.

I blinked a few times, trying to jog my memory as to who this woman was. "I'm fine, but I can't remember. . ." I started to say.

"Mae, this is Raye Porter. The nurse who took care of you when we came in." Mary Elizabeth's face reddened in embarrassment.

"It's okay. She's got a very bad concussion. I shouldn't've thought you'd remember me." A slight smile slipped across Raye's bright, cupid-framed face with her straight and long blond hair. I couldn't help but think her face would be improved if she didn't paint herself up in the pink blush and bright-pink lipstick, but each to their own.

"Then these are for you." I held the box out to her. "And Pamela."

"Why don't you give them to Pamela yourself? She's here for her night shift." Raye tugged her head to the side. "Follow me on back."

"I'm sorry I don't remember you." I felt the need to apologize because she obviously took good care of me.

"Don't you worry about it. I was with you when you weren't awake at all." Raye caught my attention. She was someone I needed to talk to about Randy Lenz.

"Was I your only patient?" I asked and leaned up against the counter when she walked behind the nurses' station. I put the doughnut box next to a beautiful arrangement of flowers. I noticed the flowers were from Sweet Smell Flower Shop in Normal.

"No. We were swamped that night." She turned and called over her shoulder, "Pamela, Mae is here."

When Pamela turned around in the desk chair sitting in front of a computer on the opposite side of the nurses' station, I recognized her.

A huge smile appeared on her face, and she got up.

"This time last night, you were out of it. You look great." She walked around the counter to give me a hug.

"I wanted to bring you guys some doughnuts to thank you for taking care of me. I know it's not breakfast, but my friend Christine Watson owns the Cookie Crumble. Her doughnuts are delicious any time of the day." I was pleased to see her and Raye admiring them.

Raye took a s'mores doughnut. Pamela took a Fruity Pebbles cereal doughnut.

"They are delicious," Mary Elizabeth noted but waved her hand in front of her to refuse one when they offered her one. "You two enjoy them. I can't thank you enough for taking care of my baby."

"She was an easy patient compared to the others that night." Raye looked at Pamela.

Pamela drew a long, shuddering breath and said, "We lost one last night, and it's heartbreaking."

"Lost one?" I asked and stared into Pamela's sad eyes.

She blinked a few times as though she were trying not to cry.

"It happens." Raye's ability to blow off Pamela's comment didn't go unnoticed. "We just hate for people to move on to the other side on our watch. Right, Pamela?"

"Yeah. Right." Pamela craned her neck to see what was beeping. "I've got to go check on a patient. I'll be right back."

"Would either of you like a coffee?" Raye asked.

"I'd love one." I clutched at the counter as though I was going to faint. Raye grabbed me.

"Mae?" Mary Elizabeth's eyes swelled.

"I'm fine. Just a little faint." I blinked a few times for good measure, hoping my performance was going to get me alone with Raye.

"Let's get you a seat." Raye took hold of my arm and helped me over to a seat outside of one of the patient rooms. Immediately, Raye dragged the stethoscope from around her neck and started to take my vitals.

"Can you get me a water?" I asked Mary Elizabeth in hopes she'd go on a wild-goose chase and take a few minutes so I could ask Raye some questions. "One with electrolytes in it. Special water."

"Of course, honey." Mary Elizabeth's worried face morphed into a determination.

After she was out of sight, I began to ask Raye some questions.

"I'm sure it's just the concussion that's making you a little light-headed. Did you take your pain pills Dr. Mel gave you?" Raye asked, still squatting in front of me.

"Not yet. I was hoping to ask you a few questions about Randy Lenz." By the wide-eyed look on her face, I caught her off guard. "I remember talking to one of his family members this morning." I snapped my fingers to act as though I was trying to recall a name. "Denise, I think is his daughter's name."

"Mm-hmm," Raye ho-hummed between pinched lips.

"I really wanted to send her some flowers for her father's death. Do you have an address?" I questioned.

"Honestly, Denise isn't a big flower fan. In fact, those flowers on the counter were to her father's room, and when we tried to get her to take them home, she told me she didn't care for flowers. She left them here for us to enjoy." Raye looked back at them. "Due to the Health Insurance Portability and Accountability Act, I'm not able to give out addresses."

"Oh, that's fine. I just felt bad, and when her sibling opened Randy's curtain to apologize for what I'd overheard, it made me really sad for the family." I had to plant a seed to grow this conversation in hope of some answers.

"She doesn't have siblings. She's an only child. I grew up with her."

"You did?" I asked.

"Yes. I had also just turned down a job there." She put her finger up to her mouth like it was a big secret. "Her dad's company is investing in this whole wellness department since he was diagnosed with heart disease. He was hiring a nurse practitioner to be in-facility, so if an employee got ill or needed anything, the nurse would be there."

"You didn't take it?" I asked.

"You don't remember, but this morning, I was offered—"

"You got the nurse manager job." It was like my memory came back to me. "I'm sorry I interrupted you."

"No. I'm glad you remembered." She tilted her head. "I was actually a little concerned when you didn't recognize me because I was your discharge nurse, and you seemed so alert and with-it. Otherwise, I would not have agreed to discharge you."

"Are you glad you didn't take the job now that Denise is going to take over the company?" I asked.

"That's why I'm glad this job came through, and I didn't have to be forced to take the job. I couldn't imagine working for Denise. She can be a little spoiled." She pushed herself up to stand. "Did you say someone from her family had opened your curtain and apologized to you?"

"Yeah. I thought it was a family member." I played it off and rubbed my head like it was hurting so she wouldn't walk off from me, and so I could keep asking some questions.

"I wonder if it was Gloria." She waved her hand in front of me. "Not that you care."

"I care. I'd rather talk about this than think about this." I pointed to my head. "Who is Gloria?"

"She was Randy's fiancé. She was in and out most of the night with Randy's lawyer. From what I understand, she and Randy had an argument before the company party." Someone called her name, and she jerked up. "Are you okay? I need to run to a patient's room."

"I'm fine." I had more questions than answers, but she did reinforce my decision to go see Gloria and also check out this lawyer.

Why didn't Denise use the family lawyer?

I got up and made my way back over to the nurses' station to wait for Mary Elizabeth. The beeps of the machines behind their counter sent chills up my spine. I turned around and noticed all of the patients that'd been brought in tonight.

Some of them didn't look very good, and my heart hurt. I was a lucky one who got to not only leave but walk out on my own in less than twenty-four hours after my car accident.

I sucked in a deep breath and gave a little prayer to my parents. I could only feel they had something to do with my safety and stopping the car from going over the cliff.

"You doing okay?" Pamela had circled back around to her desk.

"I'm fine. But I have a question." I fiddled with the flower arrange-ment next to me. "What's Dr. Mel's relationship with Raye?"

"I guess it's fine. I mean, he's a doctor, and he likes things so-so." She shrugged. "Why?"

"This morning when you and I were getting coffee, you had gone to the bathroom, and she and Dr. Mel were actually having a heated discussion."

"You overheard that too?" She got up from the desk and walked over. Her gaze slid past my shoulder. She drew in a deep breath and said, "Raye is a nurse practitioner, which means she can prescribe and give medications as she sees fit. Unfortunately, when a patient dies from an overdose of something they weren't even supposed to get, the doctors can look back in our system and see which nurse gave the medication." She pulled out her nurse's badge and flipped it over. "We have this barcode on the back, and we have to scan it anytime we get medication out of the dispensary or even open a patient's chart."

"There you are," I greeted Mary Elizabeth as she walked up all disheveled. "Are you okay?"

"I went through hell and high water to get you this water. You better still need it." She was all sorts of ornery. She pulled a tissue out of her coat pocket and wiped the beads of sweat that had formed across her lip.

"I'm good. I have no idea why I was so dizzy." I made a straight face, all without a qualm on my conscience.

If I'd not sent Mary Elizabeth off on a goose chase, then I wouldn't have gotten the clue I needed to take back to Ava Cox.

CHAPTER NINE

Mary Elizabeth insisted we head back to the campground for me to rest. She was probably right. My head was actually starting to hurt again but not enough to take a pain pill, so I'd strapped on all my warm clothes and got Fifi's leash to take her and Chester for a walk.

Hank had yet to drive past, and I knew he'd be right over, so I wondered if they'd had a break in the case. Instead of waiting on him and what he'd found out, I created a text message thread between me, the Laundry Club ladies, and Ava.

I couldn't get a whole lot out of the nurses at the hospital. I did find out that a nurse has to use their badge to get into and out of the patient's file, including when they give the patient medication. I wonder if Randy Lenz wasn't accidentally overdosed because I'd heard a conversation between Dr. Mel and Raye Porter, the nurse practitioner. Dr. Mel had told her this was going to get ugly. This was the second time I'd overheard him scold her for something. Early that morning, I'd overheard them arguing, but I just can't recall what it was about.

After I sent the text, the three dot typing symbol popped up several different times, but no one responded.

"Are you two ready to go potty?" My question made both of the dogs jump to attention and run to the door. "Poor Chester." I laughed because Fifi, who was half his size, completely ran over him. "But you don't have to go on a leash like little miss prissy pants."

He was such a good dog. He was good about staying close to me or Hank when we went out late at night. Most of the time, Hank put him on a leash because I always put Fifi on one. Fifi couldn't be trusted to stay in the light where I could see her. She would jump in the lake for a midnight swim. It was the other critters that worried me.

The winter nights—or what I considered to be winter in December, though winter didn't actually start on the calendar until January—were dark. There was very little lighting in the campground, which I'd intentionally done to preserve the natural darkness as an experience to the campers who paid good money to camp in a national park.

Tonight, the chill had settled around thirty-seven degrees with no wind. The scarf around my neck and the cap pulled down over my head helped keep the cold away. Fifi ran ahead, extending the retractable leash as far as it would go while Chester hung close to my ankles as we took a little walk up toward Dottie's camper.

There weren't any lights on, or I'd stop in to say hello. Even with the few campers I did have staying at Happy Trails, it looked like everyone had turned in for the night.

"Come on, Chester," I called to him when he went to do his business on a tree. I tugged on Fifi's leash. "Let's go to the office." Not that I needed to go to the office, but I was wide-awake, and my head felt better. It had to be the fresh and clean air, good for the soul and body.

Fifi and Chester wouldn't care about going to the office. They loved it there since they each had a bed along with all the treats in the world.

There was a glow from the office window, and I noticed Dottie was sitting in there when we walked past. She had her hair wrapped up in her pink sponge curlers, an unlit cigarette in the corner of her lip, and her eyes focused on the computer.

"What's going on?" I flung open the door.

Dottie jerked back. "Are you crazy? What's wrong with you, sneakin' up on an old woman like that." She held her hands to chest. "You gonna put me in the emergency room where you just came from."

I doubled over in laughter. The more I tried to stop myself, the harder the snorts and chuckles came out.

"Are you playactin'?" Dottie asked with a curious look in her eyes. "Are you drinkin'? What's wrong with you?" She reached down and unclipped Fifi's leash before twisting the lid off the dog-treat jar and tossing Chester and Fifi a bone.

"Oh, Dottie." I laid Fifi's leash on Dottie's desk. "I needed a good laugh."

"Well, I reckon I'm glad you got one at my expense." The back of the chair groaned when she eased back.

Dottie's phone chirped. With the bigger-than-normal font size she used on her phone, I could clearly make out Ava's name on the screen.

"Why are you getting a text from Ava?" I asked and took my phone out of my pocket. "Are y'all not texting me?"

It became obviously clear that no one had responded to my text message from earlier and that they'd taken me off the group text.

"What is going on here?" I went to grab Dottie's phone, but the old broad beat me to it. "Give me that phone." I leaned over her desk, reaching above her head where she'd thrown her arm up so I couldn't get to it.

"What's going on here?" Hank had opened the door while me and Dottie were playing cat and mouse. Chester and Fifi both scrambled toward him, one trying to beat the other for his attention.

"Nothing." I pulled my arm out of the air and tugged down the hem of my coat where it'd crept up along my torso from stretching to get the phone. "This isn't over yet," I whispered so Dottie could hear me but not Hank.

"I'm trying to keep her from being sick." Dottie made it super clear she and the rest of the Laundry Club ladies had been on their own text thread without me.

"Are y'all doing this without me?" I glared, not worried Hank was going to know at this point.

"Doing what?" Hank asked from a squatted position with both pups propped up on his leg and straining their necks to see who could kiss his face first. He tried to move his head side to side to see me and Dottie, but Fifi was just too light on her paws.

"I can't believe you. I'm fine," I told her. My jaw clenched. "This is not the end." I twirled around on my toes and headed to the door. "Let's go, Hank."

I didn't wait around to see exactly what was taking Hank so long to get to my side. With my eyes on the twinkling lights that hung on the outside of my camper's awning, I threw my shoulders back and hurried through the darkness. Not until I was halfway there did I hear Hank's heavy steps and his stern voice as he tried to wrangle both dogs, which he wasn't good at.

"Hold up." His voice pierced the silent winter night. "I've got a surprise for you."

That got my attention. I happened to love his surprises.

"You solved the crime?" I stopped and waited out of curiosity. It would make me ever so happy because Dottie and them were trying to sleuth without me.

What were they thinking? We were a team. Even though we weren't a legit investigation team, I still considered us a team.

"No. I didn't solve it yet, but we did bring someone in for questioning who might've been the killer. Come on." Hank took my hand. "Baby, you're cold." He wrapped his arm around me and snuggled me close, almost entangling our legs as we stumbled over each other, both of us laughing.

"Are you feeling okay?" His question was as soft as the winter breeze.

"I feel fine." I squeezed his hand in mine. "Now, what's my surprise? A car? I could definitely use a car." I smiled to myself when I remembered how I'd made a mental note earlier to go see Bobby Ray. Dr. Mel had told me not to get upset if I couldn't remember things that'd gone on during the day.

"You, young lady, do not need to be driving." He definitely didn't get me a car. We stopped in front of my camper, and he turned me away from it, facing the lake. "Don't turn around until I tell you."

"Okay." I gave a hard nod but tried to listen intently. "So who did you bring in?" I asked.

From the sound of the creaky metal steps up to the camper and the screen door to the camper opening and shutting, I knew he was putting the dogs inside, so whatever the big surprise was, it had to be outside.

"That nurse, Raye Porter. You can turn around now."

"You brought me Raye Porter?" I turned around and looked at him.

"This." He had a small Christmas tree in one hand and, in the other, gripped another, much larger one. He gave the larger tree a hard thump to the ground. Snow fell from its branches. "I got you a tree for outside and a fake one for inside."

"You think Raye Porter killed Randy Lenz?" I questioned and blinked a few times. "I mean, he did offer her a job, and she didn't take it, but why would she kill him? I mean, she just took the head nurse's job at the hospital."

"Seriously." Hank's jaw dropped. Even through the darkness of the night, I could see his gaze come to a rest on me. "You've been hounding me to go with you to get a tree for the outside of the camper. I bring you one, and you don't even see it."

"I do see it." I smiled through the questions I wanted to blurt out but clearly noticed the disappointment on his face. "I love it." I gave my best squeal so as not to hurt his feelings even more.

"Yeah, yeah." He shook his head and let me embrace him, his hand still firmly wrapped the tree. "You don't have to pretend. I know that look, and you're not going to let it go until I tell you exactly what." He stopped talking and drew his head back. His brows furrowed, and his eyes lowered. "How did you know she knew the victim?"

"Randy. The victim has a name." Honestly, a pet peeve of mine was hearing the dead person referred to as just a victim. He had a name. "He needs to be called by his name: Randy Lenz."

"Mae." A little snort escaped him. "I think you've gotten a little too close to this case."

"I was there. What if I did hear something when I was in my unconscious state? Maybe that man and woman killed him." I paced back and forth. "Why else would they be apologizing to me?"

I had no idea how long he let me ramble, and I couldn't even begin to repeat what was coming out of my mouth, but when I finally peered up, Hank was standing there with a blank look on his face, the tree still in his grip.

"I'm sorry." I hurried over to him. "I, um, I. . ." I clamped my lips together.

"Who came over and apologized? And you overhead Raye and Dr. Mel arguing?" he asked.

"Let's go get the decorations," I suggested. "I'll explain on the way."

Hank was eerily quiet on our way up to the front of the campground where the storage unit was located. I told him about how I'd overheard Dr. Mel and Raye behind the closed door before she came in and introduced herself.

"I swear I've heard her voice before." I shook my head.

Like an old married couple that did things naturally, Hank took out his phone and flipped on the flashlight, shining it on the storage unit lock so I could get the little key in it.

"Maybe I heard her voice when she was killing Randy Lenz." I turned the key, and the lock clicked open.

I took a step back while Hank turned off his phone light and stuck it back in his pocket so he could lift up the storage door. There was no way he wanted me to push, lift, or carry anything that was remotely heavy. They were all treating me with kid gloves, and I had to say that I didn't like it one bit.

"Then when I was being discharged, I overheard Denise tell Dr. Mel that she wanted an autopsy." I stepped into the storage unit and tugged on the string hanging in the middle to jerk the light bulb on. "Honestly, I need to invest in some new lighting in these units."

"How do you know it was Denise?" he asked.

"Well." I gnawed on my bottom lip with my upper teeth. I'd been caught. Too much talking. That was always my problem. "That's where the whole fight with Dottie comes in. You know, the one you walked in on."

I pointed to one of the boxes underneath a pile of other boxes.

Hank let out a long sigh, and I think he actually rolled his eyes, but I didn't have the time or the energy to call him out on it, especially since he'd already started to unstack the boxes so we could get the one clearly labeled Christmas in big black letters.

"Denise Lenz is Ava's new client. Ava had stopped by the Laundry Club when she saw me in there."

Hank put his hand out to stop me. "I don't need to know anymore." He picked up the Christmas box and set it aside. "We have a good case against Raye Porter, and until I can figure it out otherwise. . ." He shot me with a sideways glance that revealed I'd put doubt in his head. "Do you know who the couple of people who apologized to you were?"

"No. You didn't see them when you walked in?" I questioned because I one hundred percent remembered that was when he'd entered the room.

"No, I didn't." He sucked in a deep breath and put the box down. He ran his hand through his hair. "You can't remember what they might be apologizing for?"

"No." There was a sudden pain in my head. I closed my eyes.

"That's it." Hank put both hands on me and gently pushed me down on a couple of the stacked boxes. "You need to go rest, and we can put the tree up later."

"Just give me a minute." I scanned the storage unit, squinting at the few boxes I kept inside from my previous life. "This is the entire first half of my life." I gulped back tears. "I'm not so sure why I keep thinking about my past."

"Are you thinking about Paul?" Hank's eyes held concern.

"Heck no. That's done and gone, but that box over there is from my childhood." I'd yet to share more of my past with Hank. I'd only given him a glimpse of the few memories I had, and they were mostly about living with Mary Elizabeth and the funnier situations, like me sneaking out of the house, things that weren't too connected to me emotionally.

"For some reason, I keep thinking about my biological family." I was super careful not to say just "my family" because I'd made my family what it was today. My family consisted of not only my foster family, which included Mary Elizabeth and Bobby Ray, but my friends and the community I had built in Normal.

"I'm sure it's just part of having a near-death experience." Hank always seemed to have the perfect words for when I couldn't find them.

"Do you mind grabbing that box?" I asked.

"Not at all." Hank was eager to learn more about me. In the beginning of our relationship, he'd continually asked questions that I'd gotten good at skirting over the last fifteen or so years. "It's not too heavy."

"There's not much a girl can collect from a house fire that's salvageable." I watched him put the box carefully on the ground in front of me. I slid the lid off. "This is the only thing I took with me when I skipped town on my eighteenth birthday."

"Really?" He smiled. "I'd give anything to have known you back then."

"No you wouldn't." I took out a dirty baby's bib. "This is from my little sister, who died in the fire. She was a baby. It's still dirty." I ran my finger over the dried food.

"When social services let me go back to the house after the fire chief cleared the scene. . ." My voice cracked. I remembered exactly what it looked like from the back of the social worker's car.

I could still smell the stench of his cigar. No wonder I didn't like cigars. As soon as we rounded the curve in the old road where my home was, the outline of the fireplace was the only thing standing against the blue sky that day. I kept my eye on it as we pulled up, and I remember the social worker saying to me, *"See, nothing left. Just like I told ya."*

Hank bent down next to me. His hand was on my knee, focused on my story.

"I wanted to see for myself." I stared at the bib. "This was left. It was left right next to the burned baby high chair. I remember feeling so happy that I had found it. I walked around for about ten or so minutes, picking up pieces of whatever I could find." I reached back down into the box and pulled out photos that were half-burnt, showing only a leg or arm.

"I look at my hands, and I see my mom's hands." I showed Hank one of the photos of my mom. The top of her head was missing, but her smile was hidden under her hand. "She had crooked teeth. She always covered her smile. I thought she was beautiful."

Hank looked at the photo. He put it down and reached for my hands, taking them in his. He turned them over then looked up at me and smiled.

"Beautiful. . .just like your mom." He ran his fingers lightly across the top.

"Enough of that." I swatted his hand away. "Grab the Christmas box so we can get this tree up." I stood, leaving him squatting.

He put both his hands on his knees and let out a long sigh before he pushed himself up. "You just don't want to let me in, do you?" He wrapped me in his arms. "I know there's more in there. Maybe you should go see Tex again."

"Oh goodness. You've been talking to Mary Elizabeth." It wasn't like either of them to keep a good secret.

"She's just worried about you. She said you're chomping at the bit to drive." He had that fatherly tone in his voice. "There's no reason for you to want to leave. Even your little sleuthing is finished now that Raye Porter is in custody."

I was about to argue with him about my driving privileges but decided not to because I wanted him to tell me what exactly happened.

"But I do want to know more about the couple that came into your room and who apologized." He hoisted the box up, and we walked out.

He waited for me to pull down the door of the storage unit and fumble with the lock before we headed back to the camper.

Fifi and Chester were peering out the window of the bedroom when we got back.

"Why don't we wait to do this tomorrow?" I suggested. "It's late, and

I'm tired. How about a drink?" I knew if I got him to sit down and relax, he'd open up about the investigation.

"Sure. If you want. I'll take a water. I have to go to work early. I just want to make sure you're okay."

"I'm fine," I assured him, and I honestly felt great. I only wished I could remember what I knew was in the back of my head. It was like a tickle I couldn't scratch. Possibly, he was right. Tex had unlocked a few past memories. Why not a few recent ones?

I'd gone inside of the camper and tossed the pups a couple treats to keep them happy when I got a water for me and Hank. On my way back out, I tugged a blanket off the couch.

Hank had already made himself comfortable in one of the Adirondack chairs. I sat in the other one and pulled my legs up under me before I covered up with the blanket.

"So how did Raye do it?" I asked.

"She knew the family." He didn't tell me anything I didn't already know. "She actually didn't get the job. She's been looking to get out of the current position she's in."

"The head nurse job?" I asked. "Because she just got hired for that one."

"No. The floor nurse. She went to nurse practitioner school to have more involvement with patients, not become a nurse. That's how we think she got the potassium."

"What exactly happened with Randy Lenz?" I still wasn't clear on why he was there or what had really happened.

"According to his daughter, Denise, who is being represented by Ava Cox, her dad had been having some passing-out spells that were related to his heart. The doctors had told him the next time he did this, he was either going to die or have to have surgery." Hank zipped up his coat all the way to the top. It did feel like the temperature had been turned down at least ten degrees.

"Denise said she had pushed for her father to hire Raye because they were friends, but he told Denise he had other plans. Plans that included her taking over the company, and he was going to inform the company at the Christmas party. According to Denise, her father and his girl-friend had an argument at the party, which threw him into another one of those passing-out spells." The clouds of Hank's hot breath hitting the cold air looked like he was puffing away on a cigarette as he continued to tell the story.

"Girlfriend?" I asked.

"Yes. He had a girlfriend for years."

"Did she kill him? I mean, what was the fight about? Maybe she thought he was going to give her the company? Does Denise like the girlfriend?" I peppered him with more questions.

"Do you want to hear Raye's involvement or not?" This was the type of question Hank would throw at me when he clearly didn't want me to know any more.

"Fine." I shrugged and readjusted my blanket. "Go on."

"Denise said the girlfriend was never involved in the business, though she did live with him."

"Do they get along?" I asked and quickly shut my mouth when I saw him give me the wonky eye.

"You just asked the same question a minute ago with different words. Denise has no problem with the girlfriend." Hank stood up.

"That doesn't mean the girlfriend doesn't have a problem with Denise." I could tell by Hank's shifting and fidgeting, taking his hands out of his pocket and putting them back in, that he didn't want to discuss this with me.

"Mae, please, please." He put his hands together in prayer and shook them at me. "I'm begging you to please just focus on getting better. That's it."

"I am getting better by not thinking about having a concussion and using my brain to make it stronger." I still had this weird feeling that I'd heard something, or that there was a memory I couldn't recall buried back in my mind.

"What?" Hank put a hand on my arm. "What's that look?"

"I don't know." I looked up and gave him a slight smile so he didn't get too worked up about it. "Everyone keeps asking me if I heard anything while being unconscious, and I've heard stories about how people do hear conversations, but I don't recall any. Deep down"—I pointed to my gut—"I feel like I did hear something. I just hope it's not about my past because I'm not sure I'd be able to handle it."

"What do you want to know about your past that you don't already know?" Hank asked, a question that I honestly couldn't answer. "Maybe things are meant to stay buried. You know, to keep us from heartache." Hank tugged me close and kissed the top of my head.

Mm-hmm, maybe so. I appeared to be agreeable, but I was in no way, shape, or form going to just let sleeping dogs lie when it came to those two people who had apologized to me. I had to figure out who they were.

I hated to pull the wool over Hank's eyes, but I had to get to the bottom of my subconscious, even if it did expose Raye as the killer. There was something just not sitting right in my gut. When things didn't sit right in my gut, they were going to come out somehow. I might as well help them come out, and the only way I knew how was to see bare-chested chiropractor Tex.

CHAPTER TEN

I turned over for the umpteenth time, wishing for the morning to show itself. I didn't get a wink of sleep all night, worried about Raye Porter and if Hank had the right person. With everything Ava Cox had said, there was plenty of motive for more than one person to have killed Randy Lenz, and it seemed awfully convenient for it to have been an oversight on what appeared to be a flawless record of Raye's.

Who were those people? Were they the two people who had conveniently disappeared when Hank had showed up? Why did they disappear?

The snow had trickled all night long, just enough for a ground covering. According to the news, it was going to warm up over freezing, so the snow would melt away before dawn even arrived in all her glory.

The moon still hung in the dark morning sky and showed off the barren trees that would be full of life in a couple of months. One would think it would be depressing seeing the beautiful Daniel Boone Forest without the green leaves on the trees. Not me. I enjoyed watching the trees shed their leaves and go into hibernation while the roots and trunk secretly prepared the branches for their appearance in the spring.

It was my way of looking at things, and one thing I knew was that if

I didn't get a car and get out of here early, I'd never get to go see the two people on my list: Texas, the bare-chested chiropractor, and Raye Porter, the nurse practitioner who was being held for questioning in Randy Lenz's murder.

"It's okay, girl." I'd gotten up from the couch, where Fifi had snuggled into the bend of my leg, the blanket curled around us, to look out the kitchen window toward the only bungalow that was occupied.

Bobby Ray Bonds. If anyone else in the campground was up as early as me, it'd be Bobby Ray.

"It looks like I'm going to have to go wake him up." I turned back to Fifi.

She'd already climbed on the blanket and curled up with her eyes closed. She was still in need of her beauty sleep, and it was just as well, though she was always a good excuse when I needed to walk somewhere.

I headed back to my bedroom and headed over to the chipped dresser I'd gotten from the Thrifty Nickle after I moved to Normal and did a rehab on the camper. It was a perfect size for the small spot, and the clothes I needed fit perfectly, although it was far from the size of the walk-in closet—which was the size of my camper—that I'd had in my Manhattan apartment.

Boy, were those days gone. I laughed out loud thinking about it. In just a few years' time, I had gone from wanting all the expensive fashion for the season to the Happy Trails Campground sweatshirt I was pulling over my head.

And in no way would I've gone out in New York City with my hair pulled back in a ponytail without having it professionally put up by a very expensive stylist. Living in Normal had taught me a lot in the couple of short years I'd been here. And one of those things was to appreciate life and those you love.

"So why can't I just be thankful that I didn't die in a car wreck?" I asked myself while slipping into the pair of snow boots at the front door. A long sigh escaped me when I couldn't answer my own question. I grabbed my coat, and out the door I went.

The campground had a huge lake in the middle. There were camper lots around the lake, and some of those lots were empty pads where people could bring in their own campers while some of the campers were stationary and could be rented from me. On the far side of the lake, opposite the office and the storage units, were a few bungalow cabins that I also rented out. Beyond that and a little deeper into the woods were more paved lots for campers as well as a tent camping spot for those die-hard tent campers.

Bobby Ray's lights were out, but the glass on the pellet stove door glowed, telling me he'd put some pellets in there. It was almost time for him to get up anyways because he was the mechanic at Grassel's Garage, the only gas station in Normal. He generally opened the gas station for Joel Grassel.

So knocking a little early to get him up wouldn't be a big deal, or so I told myself. I took a step back when I heard him shuffling around and waved when he peered out the window.

"Mae? Are you okay?" he rushed to ask with a very concerned look in his eyes. "You need to go to the hospital?"

"No. No." I waved my hand in front of him. "Is that coffee I smell? I sure could use a cup."

"Yeah. It's brewing. Come on in." He walked across the open room to a floor lamp where he pulled the string to light up the room, which exposed Bobby Ray's lack of hair.

When we were growing up, his hair had gorgeous loose curls that all the girls envied. He still had loose curls, but instead, they started at the bottom of his head, and when he wore his baseball cap, which he did daily, it appeared as if he had a nice head of hair.

"Why don't you just cut that stuff off and embrace the baldness?" I blurted out.

"And you can just walk back on out that door." He moved past me over to where he'd put up a screen between the room and his washing machine.

"You're so handsome without the long hair." I just wanted him to be happy, and his was not a good look to get a woman. "I'm just looking out for you."

"In case you forgot with that brain thingy you got"—he emerged with a clean pair of blue work overalls he wore to the garage—"I'm the older of us, and I'm looking out for you, which makes me wonder why you're up and here."

I followed behind him like a little sister to the kitchen and took the full pot of freshly brewed coffee as he retrieved two mugs. I filled them and met him over at the table he'd made himself. Bobby Ray was really handy. He could do anything with his hands. He was also a perfection-ist, which would make him a great catch, except for that hair.

"Go on. I reckon you're here to lecture me." He leaned back in the ladder-back chair with one hand resting on his leg while he circled the rim of his mug with his other hand.

"Lecture you?" I laughed because clearly I didn't remember what I was going to lecture him about. "Must be the concussion, because I don't recall what it was that I'm supposed to lecture you about." I waved it off because I didn't have time to hear what he was talking about, and if I'd not already heard about it today from anyone, including Mary Elizabeth, it must've not been a huge deal. "I need a car."

"Oh nooo." A jovial laugh escaped him.

"I'm so glad you're finding this to be funny, but I've got to go see a couple of people, and you of all people know me."

"And you of all people know the wrath of Mary Elizabeth Moberly." His shoulders jumped up and down as he continued to laugh. He picked up his mug and took a drink. "You know she already called me about it."

"Since when do you listen to Mary Elizabeth?" I asked.

"On occasion I take what she says to heart, and keeping you off the street until the doctor clears that noggin' of yours is what I'm going to do." His eyes stilled, his jaw set. He was serious.

"I've never ever not had your back." I was going to pull out all the heart-tugged strings. "When you came here to live, I not only gave you a place"—I looked around for emphasis—"but I also got you a great job." I patted the jumpsuit he wore to work that he'd laid on the table.

"Speaking of work. . ." He got up and took his jumpsuit and the mug with him. "Let yourself out."

"Bobby Ray!" I yelled when he walked away, shutting the bedroom door. "I need a car."

"Not from me." His voice trailed through the bungalow.

I stood and fixated on the bedroom door with a slight bit of anger boiling up in me, in hopes he could see my frustration. When I heard the water pump turn on, I knew he'd gotten in the shower and wasn't going to budge on his stance.

I put my mug in the sink, ready to count my losses until I saw his key ring hanging by the door on the hook.

"If you don't give me a car. . ." I plucked them right off the hook. "I'll take your truck."

I opened the door, and without looking back, I quickly ran to my camper, grabbed my purse, and jumped in Bobby Ray's truck before he could even get his back dried off.

CHAPTER ELEVEN

"Good morning," Coke Ogden greeted me from behind the diner, which was located in the Old Train Station Motel, her motel. "What on earth are you doing here?"

"I wanted to grab one of your maple doughnuts and a cup of coffee before I jump on the trail to check out the frozen cascades." There was a bit of hesitation in her face. "I wanted to see it as the sun came up before the Winter Festival crowd showed up."

"Hm," she hummed.

"It was the first place I wanted to go to since being cleared from my doctor." I sat down on a stool at the counter and moved around the paper napkin and utensils so as not to lie completely to her face. "Your homemade maple doughnut is exactly what I need."

"So you got cleared?" She hurried around the counter and, with open arms, hugged me. "I'm so glad because when Mary Elizabeth cornered me and everyone else in town at the festival, it was a tongue-lashing I'd never even gotten from my own mother."

I gulped and tried to keep a game face. Luckily, she walked back around the counter.

She grabbed the hot pot of coffee with one hand and flipped over the cup on the counter in front of me with the other.

"Let me tell you that I don't take instruction from someone my age, but she put the fear of God in everyone. Shoo." Coke rolled her eyes. "I'm so glad you've been cleared. Now, what about your car?"

"I'm borrowing Bobby Ray's truck until I can get one." I used the term "borrowing" very loosely.

"Oh!" She lifted her finger in the air when a timer went off in the back. "That's the maple doughnuts. I've got to grab them out of the fryer."

For a split second, I almost decided to come clean, but then my common sense took over, and I forced myself to drink the hot coffee.

I was careful driving here. I wasn't feeling faint. I wasn't even dizzy. I even was able to keep focused on my drive over, which was on the north side of Normal.

I wasn't even this careful before my accident. If I'd been coming here a week ago, I'd have been rubbernecking all the way through downtown to see how gorgeous it was, but not today. I kept my hands on the wheel, eyes on the road, and my mind in the present, making it here without any hitches.

Coke came back through with not one but two maple doughnuts on a plate. My mouth watered at the sight of them when she sat it down in front of me. The brown glaze was thick on top and dripped down the side, exposing a little bit of the fried dough.

"Oh, Coke. I think you've outdone yourself." I picked up one of the doughnuts and flipped it over to look at the golden-brown, fried perfection.

"I think this batch did turn out nicely, if I do say so myself." She leaned her hip against the counter and folded her arms across her body. "I heard about that murder that took place while you were in the emergency room. I'm going to miss having the girls in here."

"In here?" I had no idea what she was talking about.

"Betts, Abby, Queenie, and Dottie." The edges of her brows met. "And that lawyer lady."

"Ava Cox." I suddenly realized the Laundry Club ladies had been meeting way out here instead of at the laundromat in fear they'd see me.

"Mary Elizabeth gave them a good browbeating." Coke laughed and excused herself when a customer came through the door, but not before grabbing the coffee pot and sticking a few menus underneath her armpit.

That Mary Elizabeth, I thought and watched Coke greet the customer. She seated them, gave them the menus, and filled their cups. She had this whole hospitality thing down. No wonder her entertainment barn was booked with various events like weddings, baby showers, and birthday parties, as well as many other things like the big company retreat she'd been working on for a couple of months that was booked for the spring.

I turned around and took the first bite out of the doughnut. The fresh maple syrup she used was undeniably my most favorite part of the frosting. It was delicious.

My phone vibrated at the bottom of my purse, and without looking, I knew it could be three people: Hank, Mary Elizabeth, or Bobby Ray.

Conveniently, I left my purse at the counter, picked up the other doughnut, and headed out the door without Coke noticing me.

I didn't want to have my phone on me when I headed down the trail to find the hippie camp where Texas lived, along with a few other of his followers like Glenda Russel, to name one of them.

Coke's motel was on an old farm that had several barns with the Daniel Boone National Forest for a backdrop. A couple of the barns housed horses for tourists. These horses lived better than I did and knew the trails they went on without anyone having to guide them.

Coke was smart when she bought the property and remodeled the old train station into a motel, fixing up one of the barns into the entertainment hall. She also added a tourist attraction to ride a horse on a trail, and a hiking trail that led down to the cascades.

The Cascade Trail had recently been approved by the National Park Committee, which I proudly served on. It was part of my duty to find new trails and test them out, so when Coke had actually blazed a trail herself, I helped clear it with the board as a national park trail so she could also promote it as another reason to stay at the motel or host an event on the property.

Little did I know there was a commune of hippies living near the cascades until I stumbled upon Glenda Russel, who told me how she'd radically changed her lifestyle.

Carefully I headed down the trail. Even though the snow had mostly melted, the sun had yet to pop up overhead to begin to melt the little slick patches on the ground and the icicles that hung from the barren tree limbs.

I'd seen Mary Elizabeth take a stumble and hurt herself, and I surely didn't want that to happen to me.

It wasn't like I was going to be able to make an appointment because Tex didn't live that way. Come to think of it, I wasn't even sure if he was a real chiropractor.

Regardless, I started down the trail with heavy and precise steps. The sun was coming up through the trees, but I'd already be well along before the sun filtered through the branches overhead to light my way.

There were few sounds coming from nature this time of the year. The bears had long gone into hibernation, the squirrels were getting fat and full on the nuts they'd collected, so they weren't scurrying around, and most of the birds had migrated to the south, and what few were here were nestled somewhere in a pile of leaves in the tip-tops of the trees.

Though it sounded lonely, I wasn't. I loved every season and all that came with it. Winter made it much easier to see through the trees, which I needed once I stepped off the path and into the woods that led to a clearing where Tex and his gang were up and around a campfire.

"Mae, welcome!" Glenda Russel had seen me from afar. Her olive skin seemed paler than the last time I'd seen her. But her red hair was even longer. It came almost to her waist and was pulled over one shoulder with some sort of twig tying it together near her collarbone.

Texas stood up, and boy was I glad to see he had on one of those rug-looking ponchos made out of wool. But it still seemed not enough to ward off all the cold days and nights that were upon us.

"Is everything okay?" Glenda asked as she walked closer, Tex by her side.

"Everything is good, but I need some Reiki." I focused on Tex.

The others behind them had gotten up from the fire and disappeared into the tents, leaving the three of us alone in the open field they called home.

"Then everything isn't okay if you need to dig back into your mind." Tex's lips formed a thin line across his face. "It's not the real power of Reiki that you're looking for, Maybelline. You want me to tap into your innermost memories. Am I right?"

"I had a car wreck." I knew I had to start at the beginning and tell them everything, from the time I woke up to the present where I had a gut feeling Raye Porter was not Randy Lenz's killer.

"And you think I can help you with that?"

Tex, Glenda, and I had walked back to their camp. They sat down in a chair near the campfire, and I perched on top of a rock next to the fire, shivering.

"I want to see if I can remember anything that happened while I was knocked out. From what I've been told, people who are unconscious hear things, and if I heard him being murdered, then I want to know for sure."

Tex and Glenda glanced at each other. Glenda gave him a nod as if she were coaxing him to tell me something.

"What?" I asked. "What's going on?"

"Well, Mary Elizabeth—" Glenda started to say.

"Oh my gosh!" I jumped off the rock and began circling the fire. "She got to you too. I can't believe her. She didn't leave anyone out. She thought of everyone. As you can see, I am fine." I put my hands out to my side and showed them I was healthy and of sound mind.

"Yes. You appear so, but what Glenda was trying to say"—he reached over and touched her hand—"was Mary Elizabeth had come for her appointment and made it clear that during the winter months, it was going to be hard for clients like her to come see me. So she'd come up with a solution, and Glenda was actually going to go through the trails with Rosa over to Happy Trails."

Rosa was Glenda's horse that was now part of the Old Train Station Motel horseback riding adventure. In fact, Glenda didn't really own Rosa. Rosa was Glenda's father's, who rented a stable for Rosa from Coke.

Long story short, Glenda's father died—well, was murdered—and Rosa remained Coke's possession. That was how Glenda and Tex decided to hold camp near the Old Train Station so Glenda could visit Rosa during the late hours when no one ever saw her, not even Coke.

"But as the Universe would have it, here you are, and so it shall be." Tex leaned back in his camping chair with a huge smile on his face.

"What shall be?" I stopped pacing and realized Mary Elizabeth hadn't come to see them at all about my head. "What did Mary Elizabeth say?"

"She suggested we see if we can live in a couple of your bungalows. We get covering for the winter, and you get free Reiki, and we get to see our customers there. A win-win for all." Glenda smiled and looked at Tex like it was a done deal.

"You do know there's no heat in the bungalows, right?" I didn't care if they stayed there. They kept a tidy camp here, and I imagine they'd keep a tidy bungalow. "I guess we could check to see about getting some little heaters, or maybe Henry has some." It wasn't a bad idea because the thought of them out in the cold winter months would make me worry and wonder if they were okay.

"We can figure all of that out. I'd love to have you. Plus, I think I'm going to love having you there." Out of the corner of my eye, I noticed Glenda's expression change to one not only of relief but one that told me it was she who really wanted to get out of the cold and have a solid roof over her head.

"Sounds great." Tex vigorously rubbed his hands together and blew on them a few times. "You'll need to come into the yurt over there since it's a little too cold out here this morning."

"When do you think we can move in?" Glenda walked beside me, both of us following Tex.

"Anytime is good." I smiled. "Today."

Glenda's eyes grew big, and she clapped her hands together. "Great. I'll start packing."

The excitement of her moving in had actually made me feel a little better. Maybe it was the act of kindness and giving them a home that made me joyful, but when I walked into the yurt, my life didn't seem as bleak as I'd thought it was.

"You know, I should be grateful for surviving the accident." I got up on the table after Tex patted the top of it. "But I can't help but think I heard something that is important to the case. I'm just not sure what it would be."

"Hopefully we can get you relaxed enough to drift into your subconscious." He helped me lay down on the table and pulled the thin sheet over me. He stood at the top of my head and did his silent prayer—whatever it was—and gently placed his hands on my shoulders.

He went on to babble his speech about Reiki and how it helped relieve the body of stress it'd been holding on to. I wasn't sure if I believed in this newfangled technique, but at this point, I was willing to give anything a try—almost anything.

Before I knew it, I was in a dream and wondering what on earth was going on around me.

"Listen." The voice was unfamiliar to me as he talked in a hushed whisper. *"The time is right now. Either you kill him, or I will."*

Kill him? Kill who? Not that I could truly see what was going on, but I could hear. I dialed into my listening skills to make sure it wasn't just a television show I was hearing.

"Maybe he will die. He's not even awake. Look around." There was a woman whispering now. *"Everyone in here is practically on their deathbed. Why don't we see if he slips away peacefully?"*

"He's done this a million times. Just do it. I don't care how you do it. Smother him. Accidently trip over the machine to unplug the oxygen. Just do it." The man's voice was much harsher. *"Or shoot him with this."*

Don't do it. Do not kill anyone.

"Good, good, Mae." Texas's voice brought me out of my dream state.

I blinked a few times, slowly bringing his blurred face back into focus.

"Hello there." There was a huge smile on his face, and he was bare chested.

When did that happen?

"Are you feeling well enough to sit up?" he asked and moved around to my side with his hand out for me to grab. "You had a very intense session. Do you remember any of it?"

I took his assistance and sat up. There was another person in the yurt with us. I didn't recognize her but was instantly drawn to her warm nature, soft smile, and laid-back vibe she gave off.

She was lovely with her long hair worn on top of her head in a pile of dreadlocks. Her dress was vibrant and colorfully tie-dyed, and she wore a pair of snow boots. In her lap was a drawing board, and she held pencils in her fingers.

"You gave a wonderful description of the woman. You couldn't really make out the man's features, but the earrings were amazing." The artist stood up from her chair and walked over to show me her sketch pad with the portrait she drew.

"I'm sorry." I cleared my throat as it was caught. "Who is this?" I asked about the drawing.

"I'm Meadow. I've worked with the police a few times on sketches. Most of the time, it's in situations like this when a victim goes under hypnosis." She was telling me who she was, but I was asking who person she drew was.

"It's nice to meet you. Thank you, but who is that?" I pointed to the sketch because I didn't recognize the person at all.

"This is the woman you saw in the emergency room. The one who had come over to your room to apologize. And I think you told us why there was an apology." Tex had walked around to look over my shoulder after Meadow gave me the drawing. "You said the woman and man were having a conversation about Randy."

I jerked up and looked over my shoulder because I knew I didn't tell Tex who the victim was. I'd nearly stated I thought I'd heard a murder take place while I was knocked out.

"Yes. You said his name is Randy Lenz, and these two people were having a conversation about killing him. The man wanted this woman—"

I interrupted him as my memory flooded back. "To smoother him or inject him with something." My jaw dropped, and I stared back down at the drawing. "He died of a potassium overdose." I shifted my gaze from the woman's eyes to the earring.

"I do remember her earring. It was so shiny, and I think I can't recall the man's face because her earring was like a huge spotlight when the lights had hit it just right." My mouth had gone dry. I tried to swallow.

"Meadow, can you please go to the cascades and retrieve Mae some water?" he asked, but it was more of an order.

She hurried out of the yurt.

"They think I heard them trying to kill him, and he did die." I blinked a few times. "Do you think I'm in danger?"

"I don't know, but I do know that you heard a murder take place. Were these the two who did it?" Tex shrugged and sat down on the floor, cross-legged. "Possibly, but maybe not. You did continually try to stop them, though I believe it was in your head while you heard them plotting."

"Did I say anything else?" I asked.

"Just a few times I had to bring you back when you started to go into a different story." He sucked in a deep breath and drew his hands to prayer pose. With his eyes closed, he said, "I believe it was something to do with your past. Though I don't think you should be exploring both memories all at once because when we do the Reiki, you are going from one subconscious state to the other. That's why I had to stop and call in Meadow."

"Did I say anything about my family?" I just couldn't leave well enough alone.

"You did say something about someone carrying you and putting you on the ground before you were fully awake." He bowed his head to his chest.

"Anything else?" I asked, not sure what to make of what he'd said.

"That's when Glenda came in, and I asked her to go get Meadow. It was after that I had you go back to the night of the accident and describe what the couple looked like." He lifted his head, sucked in a deep breath and raised his hands in the air before he opened his arms, letting them free-fall to his side. "All clear."

"I'm sorry, what?" My mind felt so jumbled up. I stared at the drawing again.

"Every time I Reiki, I have to clear my own energy from your energy. And keep in mind that your memories might not flood back into one long narrative. You will get bits and pieces here and there. You'll need to work those pieces like a puzzle." He pushed himself up to standing. "Thank you for your generous offer to live in the bungalow. We will be moving there soon. You wait here until Meadow comes back with the cascade water. Drink it all. It'll make you feel better."

When I glanced up, he was gone. I was left alone with the haunting eyes of the woman I knew I had to find.

CHAPTER TWELVE

"Young lady, I have a bone to pick with you." Coke Ogden wasted no time to point her finger at me and shake it. "Of all people you lied to."

"I didn't lie to you." I gasped and headed to the counter to get my purse. "I needed to go see Glenda." Quickly, I pinched my lips, unsure if Coke knew Glenda lived in the woods just beyond the property she owned at the Old Train Station Motel.

I dug for my phone in my purse to send a quick text to Henry Bryant, the handyman at Happy Trails, to tell him about our impending guests and to get the empty bungalows ready for them. I also gave him the "pretty please find some wood and head down to Deter's Feed-N-Seed to see if Alvin Deter will give me a deal on a few heaters."

"Gee, you think I don't know Glenda thinks she's sneaking into the barn at night to ride Rosa?" Coke rolled her eyes and dragged the towel across the counter in front of me to clean up the crumbs from the last customer. "Rosa has been in the best shape of her life. I knew it wasn't from the horse feed or straw I was buying down at Alvin Deter's place. And I sure knew it wasn't from trail rides because most people pick the younger horses." She sucked in a deep breath, cocked her brows, and came clean. "I started to write down everything I was giving her, down to how much water she was drinking a day. I even stopped using her for trail rides because I was thinking I found the fountain of youth."

She shook her head. "Nope. One night I couldn't sleep because I was up thinking about it. I saw a tiny little light scurrying across the field. At first, I thought it might be a string of lightening bugs, but when it happened the next night, I knew someone was going into my barn." She lifted her chin, and looking down her nose, she continued, "I went down there and hid in one of the stalls with my Smith and Wesson next to me. I sat under a horse blanket so the person wouldn't see me."

She snorted, pursed her lips, and blinked a few times before she looked over my shoulder. "I heard Glenda's voice talking to Rosa. Then I knew it was her, so I let it be." She gave a quick nod of her chin, gesturing me to look up.

"Thanks, Coke." Bobby Ray was standing behind me with Abby Fawn.

"What are you two doing?" I asked.

"Well, I came out of my house to go to work, and my truck was gone. So were you." He pointed at me with the dumbest look on his face, which was his way of trying me make me feel bad. "I had no way of talking to you because after calling you a million times, Coke here answers."

"Oh." I gnawed on my bottom lip, trying not to laugh.

"She answers your phone, and guess what, you're off on a trail. Which I knew was a big lie because I know and you know that Mary Elizabeth comes here to see that coo-coo chiropractor who is probably not licensed." He threw his hands up in the air. "I had no idea where this guy was located, so I called Abby."

I looked past him, and she shrugged.

"She said she'd come here and wait for you to come back to the diner so I could get my truck so I can go to work." He glanced up at the clock on the wall of the diner. "Now I'm late."

He put his hand out. "Give me my keys." His voice was commanding.

I turned to the counter and looked up at Coke when I noticed my purse was gone. She reached under the counter and plopped my purse on top. She reached in her apron pocket and took out my phone, sitting it on the counter as well.

"Here." I dug down and took out his keys. "Thanks."

"Thank you, Abby." He gave her a nod and smile.

"No problem, Bobby Ray." There was a weird formality to them that caught my attention. "What's that?" Abby didn't waste time asking me about the folded-up drawing I had in hand. I wasn't sure what I was going to do about it or if it was even a real person, but I knew I could bounce my thoughts off her.

"Can I trust you, or are you with Dottie still?" I reminded her of the betrayal.

"You know about that?" Abby's brows knitted. She fiddled with her ponytail as though she wasn't sure of my reaction. "It was for your own good."

"You can explain on our way to the library." I grabbed my phone and threw it into my purse along with the drawing. "Thanks, Coke." I turned to Abby. "Let's go."

After we'd gotten into Abby's car before she broke it, there were a few minutes of silence.

"Why do you want to go to the library?" she asked.

"I want to find out about potassium and Randy Lenz's company." The Wi-Fi at Happy Trails Campground was not provided by me. Campers had to use their own Wi-Fi in order to get on the internet.

The office had limited internet capabilities, which I did try to hook into when I was on my phone in my camper, but it was slow. That was why I needed to go to the library. Rarely was anyone there, and it had rapid Wi-Fi, not to mention a printer if I needed to print something.

"Not that I expect your help." I had to get in one last jab.

"Listen, Mary Elizabeth is a scary woman. She told everyone that if she found out we were helping you in any way with trying to find out about this murder or whatever had to do with any of it, she'd have our hides." Abby cried, "I'm frightened to death of that woman."

"She's all talk." I caught myself gripping the handle of the door when Abby took the curves of the road hard on the way back into Normal.

I knew she was a good driver and wasn't going very fast. Maybe it was just too soon to be driving. There was some sort of seeded fear that we were going to slide off the road. Yet it hadn't fazed me when I was driving to the Old Train Station Motel in Bobby Ray's car.

"All of us thought it was for your own good that we didn't carry on, so we all made a pact to not talk about it or tell you any clues." Abby was a talker, and she just kept going. "It's not like we found out a lot of stuff. Hank already has someone in custody, and Ava seems confident it was the nurse."

"I'm not so sure." I bent down and grabbed my purse off the floor-board, throwing it onto my lap. "I think I overheard this woman killing him when I was knocked out."

I searched through my purse and took out Meadow's drawing. I unfolded it and ran my finger along the crease to flatten it out. "This is the woman I believe came over to apologize to me. I had a memory during my Reiki session, and Tex had Meadow draw the woman." I saw Abby glance over a few times then focus back on the road. "But I don't want to tell you too much. . .unless you're going to ignore Mary Elizabeth's threats?"

"I, um, I. . ." She hesitated. "You seem fine to me."

"I am fine." I caught and withheld the smile that wanted to grow, pleased that Abby was going to help me after all. "Now, we can put Mary Elizabeth behind us and get down to business."

Abby and I ended up chitchatting the rest of the way to the library. We talked about the Winter Festival and how Betts had been working really hard with the choir. She even told me Queenie had a huge crowd while she led the strength Jazzercise class.

"She was really happy. There were a lot of new people who signed up for her upcoming class this week." Abby pulled into the library parking lot and parked.

"I love how Queenie is able to do own her Jazzercise and cater it to the revolving clientele." From what Queenie had mentioned before, she was able to offer special classes and discounts to her clients who were here for vacation. They didn't have to sign a big monthly contract or something yearly. She'd made classes available on a one-class-only basis.

"She's really doing well. I kinda expect her to open her own studio once something new comes available." Abby and I walked through the back door of the library so she could start her morning opening ritual. "You head on over to the computers and flip them all on. I'll go open the front doors."

The sound of the light switches flipping on as Abby made her way along the building echoed through the library. The swoosh of the front sliding doors opening sent in a cool breeze that traveled along the floor and circled around my ankles.

"Put on a pot of coffee too!" I yelled, even though I probably could've whispered because the library was so quiet.

The buzz of the computers came to life.

"What's your code?" I asked when I saw Abby shuffle by while pushing a cart full of books.

"Normal lib," she said over the squeaky wheels. "Let me put these books up from the overnight drop, and I'll be right over."

"I should be fine," I assured her and typed in Randy Lenz's name.

I scanned down the screen, and I clicked on the obituary. Up popped Randy's face. Not that I expected him to be my age, but I was taken aback at how old and frail he looked in the photo.

The wisps of his gray hair were sparse with more balding than hair. He had a thin gray mustache. Deep lines crowded his face, and his eyes were sunken in. I couldn't even make out any eyelashes.

Denise Lenz was the only child to Randy and Terri Lenz. There was mention of a companion, Georgia Gammon, but no mention of anything else about her. I hit the print button so I could keep the obit with me.

There were a lot of things you could take from someone's obituary. I needed his place of work, so I continued to survey the screen and found it at the bottom where it gave out his achievements over his lifetime. He had been an active donor to the American Heart Association since he had his first heart attack at the age of fifty. Any and all donations for his passing were to be made to the association instead of flowers. He left behind a host of employees who dearly loved him and "will miss all the birthday parties we celebrated" as well as the events he hosted in his company, Sinking Creek Winery.

"Winery?" How have we not heard of Sinking Creek Winery?" I asked out loud, knowing Abby would hear me.

I opened a new tab on the computer screen and typed in Sinking Creek Winery. The most beautiful winery popped up on the search.

"Catchy names." I scrolled through the wine selections. "Hummingbird Chardonnay, Bear Blush, Cascade Red."

"What are you saying?" Abby asked.

"Why haven't we gone to the Sinking Creek Winery?" I asked. "Randy Lenz owns the winery."

"That's him? That's the guy you heard get killed?" Abby's jaw dropped, and she bent over my shoulder to peer at the screen.

"Yeah." I turned to her. "Y'all didn't look him up?" I asked.

"After Mary Elizabeth scolded us, we kinda dropped it and told Ava we weren't going to help out. Honestly, it really did seem like Hank had it all squared away."

"And he might, but I just can't think that Raye Porter had anything to do with it." I flipped the tab back to look at Randy Lenz. "I know she told me she was offered the nurse practitioner position with the company but didn't take it. Only, Denise told Hank that Raye wasn't offered the job."

"Then you need to go see Raye and ask her who that woman is." Abby's attention was diverted when someone walked into the library and stopped at the circulation desk.

She was right. I had to go see Raye Porter. And luckily, the sheriff's department was located here in the business district of Normal, which was just a short walk away.

CHAPTER THIRTEEN

I walked around the courthouse, which was where the station was located, and headed toward the door that led straight to the little waiting area with the sliding glass window. Agnes Swift, Hank's granny and also the department dispatch secretary, sat there and vetted everyone who walked through the door.

"What can I help you with?" I heard Agnes call as soon as I stepped into the building.

When I reached the glass window, Agnes had already slid it open. She'd pushed herself up on her bony elbows to look past the glass and toward the door.

"Hey there." I waved at the cute, petite older woman with soft gray hair and saggy jowls.

"I was wondering when you were going to pop by." She ran her finger across the nameplate on the other side of the glass, her name engraved across the brass. She held her finger up. "Look here. Dust." She shook her head and got off her stool to open the door for me. "I swear. I told them they needed to have Betts clean every week, not just twice a month. But Jerry keeps saying how it ain't in the budget. Did you see all them people at the Winter Festival? Where is all those tourists' dollars going?" She wagged a finger in the air after she opened the door. "Maybe that's what Hank needs to be investigating." She shifted her head side to side, peering up at me. Then she moved her eyes up and down my body.

"You look good, honey." She held her arms out. "You gave us a bit of a scare, you know."

I bent down and hugged her. It felt so good. It was one of those lingering hugs where you knew the person giving it really meant it.

"I've not seen Hank so worried in my life. You know I raised that boy." Agnes was good at reminding me how much pride she took in the man Hank had become. She raised him after his parents took his sister all over the United States to chase a modeling career. Though they were back now, as well as his sister, he still went to Agnes for everything.

"You gave me quite a scare too. Don't you be doing that." She looked past me. "How'd you get here?"

"Abby. I was at the library, and well. . ." I grinned and shrugged. I whispered, "You know I can't leave well enough alone with the murder."

"You don't have to worry about being quiet. Everyone is out this morning. I bet they are at the Normal Diner having their morning meeting." She put meeting in air quotes. "Hank, he's already down at the morgue talking to Colonel." Colonel Holz was the local coroner. "I reckon they are thinking this poor girl back here is the killer." Agnes frowned. "I don't think she has the gumption to kill a fly, much less inject someone." She turned around and waved me inside of the office, where there were many open desks, a coffee pot, and a hallway. "Go on back. I'm assuming that's why you're here."

"Oh, Agnes. You're the best."

"That's what I hear." She snorted and went back to answer the ringing phone.

I was sure none of this was illegal, but I did think there had to be some formality of me seeing a person locked up. I'd gone to see people before and had to practically beg Hank, but things were so different in small towns. The sheriff's department only had one holding room. It wasn't even what you'd think a cell would look like.

When I walked down the hallway, I could hear sniffles. No doubt it had to be Raye Porter.

She was sitting cross-legged on the small cot, facing the door when I peeked into the window. Her head popped up when she saw someone was there. Her face lit up when she recognized me.

"Mae," she gasped. "Boy, am I in trouble here."

When the door buzzed, which was Agnes letting me in from her desk, I turned the knob and entered.

"I don't even know what to do, who to call, or how to get help." She blinked as the tears streamed down her face.

My head fought between two different conversations going on in my brain as I tried to focus on what Raye was saying. I watched her lips move, but the shape of them didn't match the words flowing in my mind.

I sucked in a deep breath and remembered what Tex had told me before I left him standing on the trail.

"I'm not a radiologist and certainly not a doctor. I can only see the results have been posted." Her footsteps came a little closer.

I recalled hearing Hank sobbing.

"Oh, Mae. Just open your eyes," Hank started to beg all over again. "I can't be without you. I only found you again for a couple of years."

"Oh, I'm sorry."

"Oh my!" The realization made me jump. "I just remembered you talking to Hank when I was unconscious."

"What?" Raye looked a bit disoriented.

"My boyfriend, Hank. The night I was brought into the ER. You were there, and he asked you about my MRI. You told him you weren't a radiologist." Not that this was a big deal, but I was remembering some things, and hopefully I'd remember who injected Randy with that lethal dose of potassium. Which reminded me of why I was here.

"I can't remember, but it does sound like something I'd say." She released her legs and eased up on the edge of the bed. Her hands were shaking. "I'm glad to see you're starting to remember some things. Most time people do not, but you are. That's fantastic," she said with a flat tone.

Not that I'd expect her to be upbeat in here, but wouldn't she want me to try to recall if I'd heard anything else? Maybe the real killer?

"Is that why you came by? To tell me you remember hearing me when you were unconscious?" she asked.

"Not really." I sat down next to her. "Raye, I have this thing I like to call a talent. Some people say I'm nosey, but it's been proven that I've helped solve some clues in cases like yours." I left out the murdering, shooting, stabbing, and poisoning tales so as not to frighten her off.

"I'm not sure I understand." She fidgeted. "I thought you owned a campground."

"She does." Agnes appeared at the door. "She has a knack for getting people to talk and figuring out these murders." She leaned her thin shoulder against the doorjamb. "If you listen to her, she might be able to get clues for another suspect, if you didn't do it."

"I didn't do it." Her head whipped around. She stared at me with a range of emotions coursing in her eyes. "You have to believe me."

Her lips were moving again, her eyes wide and pleading, but I couldn't hear what she said. It was like one of those foreign movies where the English had been dubbed over. The lips didn't match what I was hearing. Suddenly, a new memory took up all the space in my head.

"What is that?" the woman asked.

"I don't know. Shoot it in that IV thing." The man was a little louder this time.

I remembered there was some shuffling, followed up by footsteps.

"Hi." The voice I now recognized as Raye's had greeted that man and woman.

"I thought you were doing a shift change." The woman who'd been whispering had a full voice. "Did you tell them how he's done this a few times before, and we aren't giving up hope?"

"I did. But I came back because I thought I left something in here." This was when I'd heard Raye frantically walking around. *"Gosh. I guess I was wrong."*

"*What are you looking for?*" *the woman of the whispering duo asked.*

"*Nothing. You two get some rest. The emergency room can take it out of you. I know. I've been a nurse here for fifteen years this week. He's lucky to have you, you know. I'll see you two tomorrow.*"

"What were you looking for in Randy Lenz's room that night after you got off your shift?" I jumped off the cot and realized she definitely could've killed Randy. "What was in the syringe? Did you have potassium?"

"I. . .I. . ." Raye stammered and hopped up. She pleaded, "I didn't kill him. I swear."

"But you lied to me. You told me you knew the family, and that you had declined a job offer from Mr. Lenz, but in reality, he didn't give it you. You lied to my face." I spun around to leave.

"Don't! Don't leave. Please help me." She fell to her knees.

Agnes and I stared at each other for a few moments before I closed my eyes and let my inner voice tell me that I needed to hear her out.

Agnes gave me a little nod of approval. We'd been down this path together so many times, she was able to read my body language and knew what I was thinking.

"I didn't. I lost the syringe." Raye stood back up, this time a little hunched over, her hands out to me. "I lost the syringe," she whispered in defeat.

"Have you not told anyone?" I asked her.

"No. Well, yes. I had told Dr. Mel, and he tried to hunt it down because we can get sued over my negligence. I was giving him time. I thought Detective Sharp was going to bring me down here for questioning and I'd go home. I didn't think he was going to hold me, and I can only think he's gathering information to charge me." Her chest heaved up and down as though each breath might be her last. "I don't know what to do."

"I'm not sure you need to do anything but tell me if you knew the man and the woman you were talking to. Because I think you left the syringe in there before you clocked out, which makes me think they did it, or one of them did it." I swallowed hard because I was about to say something I thought I overheard, but who knew if any of it was true or made up? "I remember the syringe and you looking for something. I also remember before you walked back into Mr. Lenz's room."

"What? Tell me. What were Georgia and Abraham saying?"

"Georgia Gammon?" I asked.

"Yes." Raye nodded.

I gulped and took the photo Meadow had sketched out of my purse and handed it to Raye. "Is this Georgia Gammon?" I asked.

"It definitely resembles her. I'm not sure about those big earrings."

I cut her off by waving my hand in the air. "Who is Abraham?" I asked.

"He is the lawyer for the winery."

"Winery? What winery?" Agnes took interest.

"The Lenz family owns the Sinking Creek Winery. Randy has dated Georgia for years, but she started to work at the company maybe five or so years ago. He never wanted anyone to find out about them. It's true Denise's mom died years ago of cancer, but that didn't mean Randy didn't share a bed with Georgia. It just meant that no one talked about it." The little twist Raye was telling me and Agnes started to bring forth even more motives for Georgia Gammon and Abraham to be the actual killers.

"I had this memory of this woman." I touched the sketch in her hands.

"Georgia Gammon." Raye again confirmed it to be her.

"Georgia Gammon and whoever the man is that you saw with her in the ER." I was trying to be as detailed as could be so there was no miscommunication.

"Abraham Moon. The lawyer. He was with her all night in the ER. I even called Denise to tell her they were there and to find out where she was, but it went straight to voicemail." Raye gave me another good piece of information.

"Where was Denise? Have you talked to her?" I asked.

"No. Not a peep." Her eyes teared up again. "We are best friends. At least I thought we were."

"Something to ask Ava Cox," Agnes muttered.

"Who?" Raye questioned.

"Nothing. Let's stick with Georgia and Abraham." I shifted the focus back to the couple. "Are they dating?"

"Not that I know of. I think Randy would've had a heart attack." Raye slapped her hand over her mouth. She gulped. "He did have a heart attack. We were waiting for transport up to the coronary vascular care unit because the doctor hadn't arrived yet to do the emergency surgery. There were so many moving parts that night and so many patients. I had taken it on myself as a nurse practitioner with the ability to prescribe medication that I wanted Denise's dad to live. He'd been battling coronary artery disease, and the longer we waited, the less the chance of him recovering was possible. So I ended up getting all his meds ready for after surgery so I could have it all there." She closed her eyes. "Not only was it stupid, it was really illegal, but I love that family so much that I wanted to help."

"So you had the needle when you went to finish your shift?" I asked.

"Yes. I laid it in his room. I clearly remember putting in on the tray next to his bed so I could use both hands to listen to his heart and to feel his pulse." She opened her eyes. "I had clocked out, went to my car in the garage, and by the time I got back, the syringe was gone. Before I knew it, he coded and didn't make it."

"What was your argument with Dr. Mel about?" I asked.

Startled, she stared at me, baffled. "How do you know this?"

"I told you, she sniffs this stuff out. Better than an old hound dog." Agnes shifted her weight against the door.

"I overheard the two of you when I went with Pamela to get coffee." I tried not to show any emotion. I wanted her truth, the entire truth. "The only way for me to really help you is if you tell me the truth. All of it. Even the ugly parts."

"And even if it might get someone else in trouble." Agnes added a good point. "You are clearly trying not to get Dr. Mel in trouble."

"I don't want anyone to get in trouble. Dr. Mel looked up the chart and all the nurses on the floor that night that might've had a potassium load." She sniffled. "He didn't have to look too hard. I wasn't covering it up. I'd already called him earlier that night and asked him if I could be lead on Randy Lenz's case, and Dr. Mel told me I was too close to the situation."

"So that's what he meant when he told you that he knew this was going to happen or something of that nature before you discharged me?" I asked.

"Yes. Denise was so enraged that she didn't even look at me." It was like something popped into her head. Raye's eyes shifted as though she were trying to recall a memory. "I honestly don't even think she said where she was when her dad was there. She kept saying she didn't sign off on the papers, and I guess Georgia did."

"How do I find that out?" I asked.

"It would be in the paperwork. Especially in a death, there's a whole slew of parts that have to happen. I can't really remember who was on shift, but you can find out I guess." Her brows pinched.

"Pamela was my nurse when I woke up." My heart started to beat faster and faster. "Murderer," I gasped and tried to wet my dry lips.

"I didn't do it," Raye cried out.

"No." I searched my brain. "I remember saying 'murderer' when I woke up. Thinking of Pamela must've jogged it. She came rushing in and told me I said murderer. I remember Abraham telling Georgia to shoot the syringe in Randy's line."

"His PICC line?" Raye asked.

"Whoever did it injected it through the IV." Agnes spoke up. Of course she'd know. Since Normal dispatch wasn't always busy, she did have the job of inputting all the notes into the system.

"Right. The PICC line is the part of the IV to give shots and administer medication not taken orally so we don't have to poke them over and over. That's why I'm afraid someone picked up the syringe and gave it to him in his PICC line."

"Did they find the syringe?" I turned back to Agnes.

"Hank had them take out all the recycled needle-disposal boxes from the emergency room since there wasn't anyone in the emergency room that would need potassium. It's not something they give intravenously. We did find out it's really what the veterinarians give animals when they euthanize them." Agnes's words made my heart hurt.

I couldn't imagine what would become of me if I had to put my sweet Fifi to sleep. Shoving that heartache in the back of my head, I forced myself to focus. I had to finish this with Raye before Hank decided to show up.

"Nothing turned up with potassium." Agnes pulled her thin lips together.

"Do you think Georgia did it? I mean, she has been with him a long time." Raye made a good point.

"Do you think she thought she was going to get the company?" I asked. "I know she didn't cause him to have a heart attack, but it was right before he was going to announce his retirement and hand the reins over to Denise."

"Denise?" This stunned Raye, and her reaction caught me and Agnes off guard.

"Didn't Denise work for the company?" Agnes asked.

"She did but not because she wanted to. She never wanted to be in the company. Her father pretty much made her." Raye's new information gave me a good reason to go talk to Denise myself. "Randy always told Denise that she was his little miracle late in life. He pampered her, even now. Denise had everything she wanted. The only thing she didn't get to do was graduate from college with a degree she wanted."

"What did she want?" I asked.

"She wanted to be a nurse. We had big plans. We would go to college together, be roommates, and get our jobs together." Raye smiled at the memory, even snorted a laugh. "We said we'd meet twin doctors and get married, have babies, and retire on the beach."

"You have this life. You stayed true to your dream, and she had to watch you achieve that while she went to college and graduate with what degree?" I asked as the pieces of the puzzle started to come together.

"Business. She hated it. We lived together for a year, but after that, I got into new friendships with my fellow nurses. . ." her voice trailed off. "Do you think she set me up?"

"I don't know. I know people do weird things when they are jealous. The only thing I do know is that I overheard Georgia and Abraham making a plan to inject Randy Lenz with a syringe."

"You did, did you?" Ava Cox had walked up without us even hearing.

CHAPTER FOURTEEN

"Why didn't you tell me this when I asked you to work for me? Oh! Because Mary Elizabeth Moberly has the entire town scared to death to talk to you. So I make my way down here to charm Agnes Swift with a few doughnuts to see if my charm works as good as your charm, and here you are."

Agnes grabbed the Cookie Crumble box from Ava's hands. "My lips are sealed. But thanks for the doughnuts." Agnes hurried down the hall.

"Can I talk to you?" Ava questioned me and looked over my shoulder through the glass into the holding cell. She turned around and gestured to the interrogation room across the hall.

"I don't think she did it" were the first words out of my mouth after Ava had closed the door. "Look at you in your casual attire since moving here." I couldn't help but point out that Ava was no longer in those formfitting pantsuits all buttoned to the tip-top of her chin. "I like the sweater and khakis."

"Honestly, Mae, must we go through this dance after all these years? I asked you to look into this case, and you have, but I've not heard from you. Yes, Mary Elizabeth is a tad bit frightening, but I know the Mae West fighter, so I gave you the benefit of the doubt. And I was right." Ava still had her big, heavy briefcase, and she plopped it on the table.

She bent down and rolled the combination on the small silver wheels to unlock it.

"I guess I'm saying that your client could possibly have killed her own father." I smirked when she gaped at me like I had five heads. "Oh, I feel like I've got two brains up there rattling around, but I'm clear on what I heard when I was unconscious now that I did Reiki. Plus Raye gave me some insight on her best friend, Denise Lenz."

"I'm listening." Ava sat down with her hands neatly crossed and resting on the table in front of her.

"Denise never wanted to take over her father's company. She didn't even want to work there. She wanted to be a nurse just like Raye." I pointed in the direction of the holding cell. "In fact, Denise didn't even show up at the hospital the night her father passed."

"Then how did she kill him?" Ava smacked the table. "Let me guess." She put the pads of her fingers on both sides of her temple. "Her hatred for him handing over a half-billion-dollar company upset her so badly that she used her psychic ability of mental telepathy to kill him."

"No. But she did use her ability on Georgia Gammon." I took out the sketch and placed it on the table in front of her. "Denise was well aware of the affair her father had with Georgia before her mother had died. He only introduced Georgia to the company five years ago, which gave her a job. Georgia thought she was going to eventually take over the company. I can't help but wonder if Denise told Georgia before the party."

As the scene played out in my head, I remembered someone telling me that Christine Watson had actually catered the eggnog for winery company Christmas party and put her on my list to visit.

"Denise hated Georgia and her father for their affair. Denise didn't want to get the company. But she never saw her father's death coming. It just all played out like she was the puppet master." I smiled as the clues came together. "Her father had gotten so worked up that he had a heart attack. Georgia appeared to be the grieving partner and went to the hospital. They all knew Randy's heart probably couldn't make it through another heart attack. That's why Denise sat back and didn't hurry to the hospital to give any sort of clearance on her father's medical care, and I would assume she's his power of attorney?"

"She is," Ava confirmed with a straightlaced face.

"And if he made it through, the paperwork still hadn't been signed for her to take over because he was going to do it that night in front of the company at their Christmas party, once again pushing Denise's hand into something she wanted no part of." I paced back and forth.

"This sounds like one of those mystery novels you and the Laundry Club ladies love to read." Ava rolled her eyes.

"Then if he didn't live, Denise was free at least, but she'd already planted the seed in Georgia's head, so when Georgia saw the syringe, she injected it like Abraham told her to." I tapped my ears. "I heard them when I was unconscious. He told her to do it."

"And how does Georgia killing Randy have anything to do with Denise?" Ava asked with an amused tone. "I really want to hear this."

"Her words against her father were the weapon that Georgia needed to put an end to his life and her suffering as the other woman for good. Denise knew it would drive Georgia mad, and she sat back and waited until the next day to come to the hospital because she knew her words would marinate in Georgia's head, enough for her to do something about it without Denise getting blood on her own hands." I brushed my hands together before I took a bow.

"You clearly need to be a member of the local theater with that performance." Ava laughed and gave a little clap. "How do you know Georgia thought that?"

"I don't know, but it all sounds good."

"It might all fit together in that little head of yours, but until the syringe is found and any more facts are presented, Raye Porter is going to go down. Denise Lenz is fully ready to see to that."

"I'm only asking you to give me a week or so. With this concussion, I have limited mobility as in travel. I can't drive, but as soon as I get cleared tomorrow, I'll go visit Georgia and the winery lawyer so I can see exactly how they react." I knew Ava wanted a tightly locked case to win, and she would give me the time.

"Four days. If you solve this as you think you will, then I'll double your fee." She held up four fingers as she pushed herself out the chair. She closed the briefcase and gingerly picked it up. "Four days. I look forward to you stopping by the house."

She walked out, confident that I wasn't going to get the job done. Well, she obviously didn't know Mae West.

CHAPTER FIFTEEN

"Four days," I continued to mutter under my breath as I stormed over to the Cookie Crumble Bakery, which was also located in the business district.

When Christine Watson and her sister had opened the Cookie Crumble, there weren't many buildings available to rent or purchase for living. It didn't hurt her any being away from downtown, though, because her parking lot was always filled, and there were always customers in the bakery.

"You're here." I walked in, a bit shocked she was here. "I needed to visit you and was in the area, so I popped in to see if you were here instead of the festival booth."

"I'm here." She handed a customer their order at the counter. "Thank you so much. Enjoy your stay in Normal." She came around the counter, and we hugged hello. "It's my sister's turn to be at the booth. I about froze my you-know-what off." She smiled. "What were you saying to yourself on your way in?"

"Huh?" I was all sorts of confused.

"I'm sorry." Her brows furrowed. An empathetic look crossed her face. "Are you feeling okay?"

"This?" I snorted and pointed to my head. "I'm fine."

"Then you weren't talking to yourself when you were walking in?" she asked.

"Oh, that." I couldn't contain the grin. "I'm up for a challenge from Ava Cox, which is exactly why I'm here. The guy murdered at the emergency room—" I was going to continue, but she started talking.

"Mr. Lenz. It's awful." She drew a hand to her chest. "He was so nice, and he gave the biggest tip I've ever had for catering."

"That's why I'm here." I reached out to touch her arm and to make that personal connection before she shot me down. "He was in the ER bed next to me, and I overheard a few of his employees plotting to kill him."

Christine ripped the hairnet off her brown hair. The freckles on her face grew long as her jaw dropped. "You know, I was serving up that eggnog, and he asked me to put a little more liquor in it than normal." She waved her hand for me to follow her behind the counter, where she quickly took an order as we walked. "And those people love to drink. I mean, I knew it was a winery and all, but let me tell you, wine didn't get the floodgates of their gossip going. It was the eggnog. They kept coming back for more and more."

She slid open the glass counter, plucked two parchment papers from the box, and grabbed two apple fritters for the customer before putting them in a Cookie Crumble Bakery to-go bag. "It'll be four dollars." She handed the bag over with one hand and slid the door back with the other then moved down the counter to meet them at the register. "They were excited about the big announcement Mr. Lenz was going to give during his Christmas speech. Apparently, he was a great boss who gave generous bonuses to everyone, even to the young help who pick the bad grapes off the vine."

Both of us paused while another slew of customers came inside.

"It's getting colder out there." Christine shivered. "Take a look around, and I'll be right with you," she told the customers.

She pulled me to the side. "You do know that I only made my special Kentucky eggnog, not the one I made for the festival, right?" she questioned.

"I don't even know the difference." I shrugged.

"Oh, the Kentucky eggnog has bourbon in it." She gave an evil grin. "When a little bourbon gets in the veins, people let loose." She did a little dance gig. "There was this one lady who kept coming back, saying she was so nervous about the big announcement since she knew it was about her. Then—" Christine looked over my shoulder as soon as the bell over the door rang again, and more customers piled in. "I saw her and Mr. Lenz go out the door of the reception, and when they came back in, she was crying."

"Was she his daughter?" I asked.

"Denise?" Christine shook her head. "No. Some older lady. But Denise had come over and was laughing, saying something about her mom getting even or something."

"How did you know Denise was his daughter?" I asked.

"Because she told me. She kept coming back for more booze. She actually didn't get to stay for the announcement because she was so drunk. She literally passed out." This was good information, but it clearly made me think Denise didn't do it, which blew my theory out of the water.

"Did anyone see her pass out?" I asked.

"Her dad, Mr. Lenz." Christine sucked in a deep breath and surveyed the customers to see if they were ready. They all appeared to be looking and helping themselves to her free hot-coffee bar. "He had his lawyer come over and take her out. He looked really upset that she wasn't going to be at the announcement. He even told me this when he came over to get a refill on his eggnog."

I opened my purse and took out the sketch and handed it to Christine.

"That's the woman who was crying." Her eyes grew. "Where did you get this?"

"Long story, but she had been Randy Lenz's mistress for years before Denise's mom died, so that explains Denise telling you that about her mom. And the big announcement. . ." I swallowed. "He was going to retire and give the company over to Denise, who didn't want to work there. So I bet he told Georgia that he was going to give Denise the company, and I bet she thought she was going to run it."

"Oh, Mae." Christine gasped. "Do you really think so? This lady killed him?" She peered at the sketch again before a customer cleared their throat. "I've got to go." She took a couple quick steps to move back behind the counter. "If I remember anything, I'll call you. And be careful out there. No more wrecks."

No more wrecks? The irony. This thing with the Lenz family was an entire train wreck, and the clues were in the eggnog. It sounded as if Christine Watson had discovered a truth serum instead of an alcoholic Christmas cocktail.

"There you are," Abby greeted me from behind the reference desk after I made my way back to the library. "The ladies called. We want to give you a peace offering by having lunch."

"Peace offering, huh?" I waited for her to smile. "Y'all think feeding me is going to make that happen?"

"I think so, plus discussing the murder with you and our little notebook." She grinned, knowing she had me on the hook.

"We'll see what's for lunch." I winked and rubbed my stomach. "I'm starving. I was just at the Cookie Crumble, and smelling all of those delicious homemade pastries made me hungry."

"Then let's go." Abby got up.

I waited by the front door while she said something to one of her employees. I went over everything Christine had told me. The more I thought about it, the more I believed Georgia and Abraham had gone through with their plot to kill Randy Lenz.

CHAPTER SIXTEEN

I t took a little more time for us to drive downtown and park in the Laundry Club parking lot due to the traffic from all the tourists and townsfolk arriving for the festival. I was so happy it was a big hit and really hoped it would continue each year. If I was still on the board this time next year, I'd make it happen for sure.

"Everyone is smiling." I loved seeing the joy our cozy town brought to people. "I had no idea it would've taken off this way."

There were big barrels around the grassy median with small fires. In a couple of areas were more carolers. Kids were at the s'mores station, roasting their marshmallows while their parents stood behind them, talking to other parents. Some couples strolled hand in hand. And even Blue Ethel and the Adolescent Farm Boys had taken the stage at the amphitheater to give a live performance.

"If I just left well enough alone, I could be out there smiling and eating, having fun," I grumbled and turned to stare out the windshield as Abby pulled into a parking spot reserved for the Laundry Club.

"You can. We have tomorrow, and you have to go to the Normal Baptist Church performance tomorrow," Abby reminded me.

"Hopefully I can drive myself." I sighed and pulled on the handle to get out.

"Bobby Ray said he was finding you a car." Abby's words trailed behind me.

"What?" I looked over the hood at her and pulled my cap down to cover my ears from the cold. "He did? When?"

"It was. . ." She hesitated then pointed. "Here comes Dottie." Abby waved enthusiastically. "Dottie! Dottie!"

Dottie gave a little nod and took one last puff of her cigarette before she bent down and snuffed it out on the sidewalk, sticking the butt of it in the container Betts kept outside of the Laundry Club for the patrons who smoked before entering.

"Well, she wasn't too happy to see us." Abby laughed.

The Laundry Club was dead. No one was doing laundry because they were all having fun at the Winter Festival.

"Did y'all know Christine Watson had two separate eggnog recipes?" I was still thinking about the Kentucky eggnog.

Queenie French was sitting on the couch with Betts when we walked in. Betts was busy taking food out of the paper bag from the Normal Diner. I joined them. Abby went to the bathroom. Dottie was standing up, looking over the food.

"We got your favorites." Betts tapped one of the plastic containers. "Brown beans, fried cornbread, pimento cheese sandwich." Only, when Betts said "pimento cheese," it sounded like "puhmennuhcheese." "And a slice of chess pie."

"Y'all are really trying to butter me up after you stabbed me in the back." I tried not to let the drool show too much. The sound of chess pie made me all sorts of happy.

"I told you." Dottie was in a mood. "We were doing it because we want to make sure you're okay."

"Dottie, thank you, but I'm fine," I assured her and patted her leg when she sat down next to me. "I promise all of y'all I'm fine." I wasn't sure how I could make it any clearer.

"Of course you are." Queenie nodded in agreement. "Let's eat. I'm starving."

Betts smacked Queenie's hand away. "I know you've been hosting a lot of new classes and working out a lot, but Mae is the guest of honor," Betts scolded Queenie. "Where are your manners?"

"It's fine." I reached into my purse and took out the notebook. "Why don't I tell you what I've found out while you guys get your food? It's fresh in my head, and I think we all need to hear it because I'm telling you that I don't think Raye Porter killed Randy Lenz."

While Dottie, Queenie, and Betts filled up bowls of soup beans and plates of the side items, Abby took the notebook, and I stood up, pacing back and forth so I could remember everything.

"I had originally thought Raye had a motive but not as strong as the others. I overheard Georgia and Abraham, the lover and the lawyer, plotting to kill Randy Lenz or at least wanting to inject him with the syringe. I also know Raye had left the syringe in the room." I paused to collect the photo of Georgia out of my purse and let Abby catch up with the note-taking.

"How did Raye get the syringe? Seems fishy." Queenie slapped butter on her piece of cornbread.

I quickly told them how Raye had been a friend of Denise all her life and up into college.

"Now at first, I thought Denise actually got even with Raye for having the life she wanted by setting Raye up as the killer. And Denise would have the ultimate payback for her mother by killing her father in the process, getting away with murder." I wagged a finger when I noticed all of their eyes were on me, and they all had that look on their faces that they agreed. "Not the case. Christine Watson told me she had served the Kentucky eggnog at the party where Denise got so drunk, she passed out. Randy Lenz had his lawyer carry a passed-out Denise away, which means Denise was in no shape to go to a hospital and kill her father."

"And it does make sense that she showed up the next day and not that night." Abby made a good point.

"How does that make Raye clear? She was still there, right?" Queenie asked.

"Unless she left." Dottie slurped some bean soup off her spoon.

"She told me she clocked out and went to her car, where she remembered she'd forgotten the syringe." Which reminded me to answer Queenie's question. I stood in front of Queenie. "Which brings me back to your question on where she'd gotten the syringe of potassium that ultimately killed him."

The three of them edged up a little closer on the couch.

"Potassium is used in small doses for patients who've had heart surgery." I didn't go into the exact potassium because it would only confuse them. "And since Raye considered Randy Lenz a very personal matter, since she still believed her and Denise were friends, she wanted to take his open-heart surgery case, which was what he was waiting on at the hospital. The problem was he wasn't stable enough to move from the ER, and they were waiting for the cardiologist to show up. Still." I put my hands out and started to walk again. "Raye told me that she was trying to get all his medication prepared for after the surgery when she came in the next day."

"Isn't this all kinda illegal?" Abby asked.

"I'm sure it is, but I'm not the hospital board of ethics. I'm sure all of that will be taken care of. All I care about is getting the memories sorted to what really happened to Randy." I knew that if Raye didn't kill Randy, there was going to be some sort of repercussion to her job, possibly getting her license suspended or worse, revoked. "Which brings me back to what I heard Georgia and Abraham discussing while I was knocked out."

I walked over to the table and scooped out a bowl of beans from the diner's to-go container and told them how I'd heard Abraham, or who I assumed was Abraham, give him the shot.

"That's fishy they'd apologize to you. I mean, if they thought you overheard them, don't you think they'd have tried to kill you?" Betts asked a question that made me all sorts of scared.

"Yes, but Raye had come in to get the syringe, and she couldn't find it. I think somewhere between me hearing them and then me hearing

Raye come in was a lag time that I can't remember. When they saw Hank come in to see me after I woke up, I think they didn't want to be seen, so that's why they slipped out of my room."

"So we're thinking Georgia and Abraham did it?" Abby asked for clarification.

"But what would be the motive?" Dottie nibbled on a piece of cornbread.

"I think Georgia thought she was going to get the company, and when he told her at the party before the announcement that he was going to have Denise take over, it was her final straw." I planted the seed.

Betts ran with it. "Then when he went to the hospital, she arrived as the grieving girlfriend, and as the night went on, Abraham told her the papers weren't signed. They made a side deal. Do we know who would be in charge if he died and had not signed the papers for his daughter to take over?" Betts had completely gone in an opposite direction.

"No. But I want to go to the winery tomorrow and snoop around." I grinned.

"I can ask Ava to look into the last will Randy had when I talk to her in the morning to give her an update." Betts readily took on that role.

"I can also get a list of employees who were at the Christmas party before we go in the morning so if they are at the winery, we can ask them some questions." Abby took on that task, and I had no idea how she would get this list, but she had connections we didn't know about.

"I did go in there once to give them a demonstration on how to keep fit and healthy when they started looking into making their employee facility a wellness center. It was just a few months ago. I can get us in by telling them we are following up." Queenie had the most brilliant idea.

"That's brilliant." I clapped my hands together. "That will get us in the door."

"From there, we can meander around." Dottie had that look of excitement in her eyes.

"Do you think you can get us some Jazzercise clothes?" I asked.

"What time are we leaving?" Queenie asked. A devious smile curled along the edges of her lips.

It was settled. We were all going to pile into Betts's van and head to Sinking Creek Winery, all before they took me to my doctor's appointment so Dr. Mel could clear me from the concussion.

CHAPTER SEVENTEEN

Dottie took her good ole sweet time driving us back to the campground, which was unusual, but what caught my attention even more was how she didn't smoke one cigarette between the Laundry Club and Happy Trails.

"I'm so proud of you." I unzipped my coat with just a couple of miles left to drive. The heat was turned all the way up to high, and I felt like I was being cooked like a Christmas turkey. "You've not smoked a single cigarette on the way back home."

"The way I see it"—she tapped the wheel with a nervous energy—"I don't want to hurt that noggin of yours anymore."

"My noggin is fine," I mocked and smiled. "But I do appreciate you not smoking. And thank you for driving slowly."

A sudden pain shot up my arm, and I looked down at my hand. Without realizing it, I'd been gripping the door handle even though I knew Dottie was taking it slow on the curvy roads. I gulped and forced myself to let go.

"I can tell you're a little tense." Dottie's eyes shifted from the road to my hand, where I was working it by opening and closing it.

I slipped the hand under my leg.

"Don't need to hide nothin' from me." She focused her gaze back on the road and lifted her chin in the air. "I can see things without you having to say. I can tell something else besides this murder is on your mind too."

I smiled. There'd been a time I'd tried so hard to keep my emotions in check and tried to keep them buried deep, but over the past couple of years, my trust in people had gotten somewhat better. The poker face I'd perfected had practically faded.

"I have been having some memories of my past. At least, I think they are memories." I swallowed, not sure if I should confide in Dottie or even Hank. Possibly neither.

"Now listen here." She wagged a finger at me before she turned the wheel toward the driveway that led up to the campground. "If that Tex is puttin' stuff in your head, then he's gonna have to deal with me."

"He's fine." I'd completely forgotten to tell her about Tex and Glenda moving in. "Speaking of Tex. . ." I sucked in a deep breath, ready for the tongue-lashing she was going to give me for not making them pay.

Though I was the owner, sometimes it felt like Dottie was the rightful owner or at least should be. She knew all the ins and outs of the campground. She had all the financial numbers in her head when I had them on paper. Plus, she knew how to talk to people. Half the time, she was sarcastic, but she came across as funny.

"What on God's green earth. . ." Her voice faded, her body stiffened, and her hands clenched. "Is that Glenda Russel?"

I looked up, past the storage units and past the office, to where Glenda and Tex were ice-skating on the pond. You guessed it. Tex was shirtless.

"And is that naked Tex?" Dottie's jaw dropped. "Mae West, what have you done?"

"You're gonna run off our campers with them yahoos in here. That man is gonna catch cold as sure as I'm driving this here car." She jerked the car to a stop when we'd pulled in the middle of the road between her camper and mine.

"I-I. . ." I fought for words, still in shock seeing Tex spinning around like a true skater you'd see in the Olympics. "Honestly, I was thinking they needed a place to live for the winter. I got to wondering if I needed —" I was going to tell her about my memory, but she cut me off.

"Do not let your mind wander too much. It is too small for you to let it out alone," she snarled then looked over at me. "I hope your doctor don't give you a pass to drive tomorrow because now I know you got a major concussion that ain't one bit fixed."

"Healed," I muttered under my breath and grabbed my bag from between my legs.

"What?" She spat. "I didn't hear what you said."

My phone buzzed in my purse, and I dug around to find it.

"Is that Hank? You need to tell him what you've done. Let a bunch of tree huggers who're doing all sorts of voodoo on you in here for free. Free!" She threw her hands in the air.

"It's Agnes. She said Hank has stopped the transport of Raye Porter." I smiled, gripping my phone. "Maybe, just maybe, we can really dig into more clues in the morning."

Dottie gave me the wonky eye with pinched lips. I could tell she liked what I said but was too mad to tell me.

"It's okay. All of this will be fine." I patted her arm.

"If you think we're feeding these people for Christmas supper, you're nuttier than I originally thought when I first met you." She tucked the unlit cigarette in the corner of her lip and turned her head to glare at Glenda and Tex.

Glenda waved. Dottie crossed her arms and shoved her hands up under her armpits.

"You should be ashamed. Glenda has seen you like an aunt all these years, and you treat her this way." Dottie was a lot of things, but she was also softhearted and kind under all those hard layers of her heart.

Dottie and Paulette, Glenda's mom, had been best friends for years before they'd had a somewhat past incident that she didn't like to revisit.

"I just can't believe she's following in Paulette's footsteps. Didn't she learn how it made her mama crazy?" Dottie huffed and puffed.

I wasn't going to touch that conversation or situation with a ten-foot pole. "I'm going to say one thing." I put my hand on the door handle. "People can change. I'm proof." I opened the door.

"What are you doing? We aren't at your camper." She jerked around and stared at me.

"I'm going to walk. I need the fresh air." I didn't really need the freezing fresh air, but I knew it would make her think about what she was unfairly saying.

"You're gonna catch cold!" she yelled as soon as my feet hit the blacktop. "Zip your coat!" she hollered before the door shut behind me.

"Did you find everything okay?" I asked on my way down to the lake to greet my guests, even though Dottie wasn't going to see them that way.

I did. They deserved to be treated as guests, though I wasn't having them pay. They were still people and good people. I ignored Dottie's erratic backwards driving, going back toward her camper.

"We love the pellet stoves." Glenda waved again with a big smile on her face.

"Pellet stove?" I questioned and looked over to the bungalows, wondering if they'd accidently wandered into Bobby Ray's place.

Henry's golf cart was parked in front of one of the bungalows, so I headed that way.

When I glanced at my little yellow camper, Fifi was in the front windshield, wagging her little poodle tail so hard her entire body was shaking. Of course, I went into my camper to get her before going to see what Henry was doing.

"You are the best." I picked her up when I made it inside, where she was dancing around, so happy to see me.

Her little tongue gave me a ton of kisses.

"You always love me no matter what." I snuggled her close. "I love you no matter what."

She wiggled and jiggled so I could put her down. She knew what was next. A treat.

I opened the treat jar on the counter and handed her one. While she devoured it, I opened the drawer under the captain's chair of the passenger side of my camper, and I took out Fifi's sweater. It was adorable. I'd gotten it from Smelly Dog the last time Fifi was there for a grooming. Ethel had just gotten them in, and I knew they would go fast. Everyone put dog sweaters on their pups around here, and the cold temperatures called for them.

Fifi loved her pink sweater with the red and green puff balls around the neck. There was a green glittery Christmas tree on the back with a bell as the star. Every time she wore it, the bell would ring with each step. It was the cutest thing. She was the cutest thing.

"Let's go pee-pee." I called for her and bent down. She stood still to let me put the sweater over her neck and her front legs into the holes. I brushed down the back of the sweater and tugged at the end.

She knew the routine as she rushed over to the door and gave it a little scratch.

"Okay." I left my keys and purse on the counter.

She darted out the door, and since it was still daylight out, I didn't have to worry about putting her on a leash. Really, I only put her on a leash so other critters didn't get her at night.

Bobby Ray had pulled up to his bungalow while I was inside of the camper. It was time to apologize to him for taking his truck this morning. He'd rushed off so fast from the Old Train Station that I didn't get to make good with him.

Henry had the plastic cover that enclosed the golf cart zipped up. I could feel the heat coming from the inside. It was a super nice golf cart that I'd gotten after the first winter I was here. Henry was older, and he didn't need to be out in the cold. He certainly wasn't going to retire, so to keep him happy, I'd gotten him the fancy golf cart.

Outside of the bungalow door was a bucket of pellets, and the door was cracked.

"Knock, knock." I tapped on the door to let Henry know I was out there, but Fifi had already run in, so I was sure he already knew. "What's going on?" I pushed the door the rest of the way open.

"I see she finally got home." Henry was sitting on the ground with his tools around him. Fifi had already made it into his lap. "This little girl has been sitting in that windshield all afternoon. I almost went up to the office to get your spare key to let her out."

"You can anytime." I didn't keep anything near and dear in the camper. Actually, I didn't have anything near and dear, only the relationships I'd formed since living in Normal.

"Thanks for the few minutes notice," he whispered fiercely under his breath.

"I'm guessing they were here pretty quickly?" I asked and walked over to see how he'd put the venting through the wall. "I felt bad for them out there in the woods, and we don't rent these anyways."

"Well, you can now." Henry shooed Fifi off his lap, and he pulled back up on his knees. "Alvin said to take them, and you and him can square up during kayak season."

"Did he?" My brows raised. Squaring up with Alvin Deters meant he had some sort of business plan in mind.

He ran the kayak service for me when the weather allowed. He also gave kayak lessons to my guests or anyone who wanted them. Just over the past six months, I'd acquired the new business, which was just off Red Fox Trail, one of the many trails we had.

The trail was a nice hike down to the rolling river, where there was great kayaking and white-water rafting. After I'd taken over the business that was already there, I had zero knowledge of how to kayak or white-water raft, nor did I want to learn.

After I'd heard Alvin had been a champion kayaker, it was only natural for me to add more to his plate, even though he owned Deter's Feed-N-Seed and was the local bank's president. Kayaking was his passion, so he made time to take my offer, which was what led me to believe he had something up his sleeve if he gave me four pellet stoves to go in the four empty bungalows.

"Well, now we can rent them out." It was a quick decision I would make and incorporate into the business plan for the next year.

"I swear, Mae West." Henry shook his head and tried to hide the grin that was growing, exposing his missing two front teeth. "You're the smartest woman I know." His nose was already large, but it grew as his smile did.

"You are the handiest man I know." I winked just as someone behind me cleared their throat.

"Henry, don't let her sweet-talk you. She's said I was the handiest man she's ever known." Bobby Ray stood in the doorway of the bungalow.

"Pay him no attention." My nose crinkled as a huge smile spread across my face when Henry and I caught eyes. "Thank you." I made sure to thank Henry again before I got up to see Bobby Ray.

"Me and you have some business to attend to." Bobby Ray narrowed his eyes at me.

"Sure." I shrugged and breezed past him, on my way outside with Fifi tagging along behind me. "We can go to your place."

"Honestly, Mae, who are these people?" Bobby Ray asked in a hushed voice as we walked past the campfire surrounded by a few of Texas's followers.

"They are people who need a place to stay that's warm." I patted my leg when I noticed Fifi was straying over to them. "Fifi, come."

Bobby Ray rushed up next to me. I could feel him staring at me in the way that he did to make me uncomfortable enough to talk. Not this time. I pinched my lips together to stop them from flapping.

"You, of all people, to question me on who I help? You help people all the time." So my mind completely took over and didn't listen to my lips.

"Oh, I remember very well how I've helped you all my life. From the forged high school diploma."

Slowly, I sucked in a deep breath, clenched my fists, and turned around to see he'd taken on a more scathing look, the I'm-going-to-put-Mae-in-her-place face.

"You said we were never going to mention that again." My nostrils flared as the anger welled up inside of me.

"You know, Mae." He jerked his keys out of the pocket of his jacket and unlocked the bungalow door. "Sometimes you have to be reminded of your past to realize just where you come from. I understand your giving heart. But do you really know these people?"

The warmth of the inside of the bungalow felt good on my cold hands, but my cheeks were on fire from Bobby Ray bringing up my past. "I'm not going to let you hold that diploma over my head. We are going to finish this off right here and right now, because I've felt like I've made up for that over this last year or so since you moved here."

Granted, what Bobby Ray did for me was beyond illegal, and I honestly wouldn't be here in this position today if he'd not forged all of Mary Elizabeth's signatures when I was a senior in high school, actually excusing me from school when I was skipping school. But the real thing he did for me was forge a high school diploma. Since I didn't technically graduate, I'd needed a diploma to apply for the airlines to become a flight attendant.

"Without that job, I'd not have met Paul West or gotten married, only to be taken for any sort of savings I did have when he wrapped me and everyone else in the world, or so it seemed, into his little Ponzi scheme, leaving me a run-down campground, which just so happened to be Happy Trails, where I took in Bobby Ray, gave him a place to live and a job. End of story." I stomped my foot.

"Here." Bobby Ray took out another set of keys from the pocket of his jacket before he peeled it off. "I got you a car."

"What?" I gasped and broke out in tears. "You did?" I cried.

"Oh, Mae, don't cry." He walked over and curled me into his big, snuggly, and smelly work overalls. "I'm still your big foster brother no matter what. When I think people are taking you for a ride, I get a little bit brotherly."

"Is that a word?" I asked and hugged him tighter before I let go. "How much do I owe you?"

"For the car?" He shook his head as he walked over to his pellet stove to start it up.

There were a blanket and pillow on the floor in front of the stove. It made me wonder if the nights were too cold for his bedroom and he had to sleep on the floor. I didn't want to say anything because he'd get defensive and tell me he was fine, so I made a mental note to see if there was anything Henry could do to make the bungalow a little more insulated for Bobby Ray.

"Not a thing. You let me live here for free when you could be charging a guest. It's the least I could do. It's not new by any stretch of the imagination, but it has a good engine in it. It's a solid little four-door."

It didn't matter what make or model the car was. I knew that if Bobby Ray approved it, then it was good. "Are you sure?" I asked.

"Yep. It came into the shop. The owner was going to trade it in for a new car, and I asked him what he would take for it." He held the keys out in his palm. "We wheeled and dealed. I did it with you in mind. To keep you safe. You scared all of us the other night. By the way, do you remember me coming to see you?"

"No." I shook my head.

"Good." He headed to the kitchen, where he grabbed a beer from the refrigerator. He held one up for me. I shook my head. "I'm glad you don't remember because I might've told you some sappy things you don't need to know."

"You love me. You love me sooo much," I trilled.

"I do love you, kiddo." He rolled his eyes and popped the top of the beer. "So what's going on with these people?"

"That's Tex."

Bobby Ray's eyes lit up. He almost spit out the beer in his mouth. "I should've recognized him with no shirt on. I just figured he was hyped up on some sort of drug."

"Oh my gosh." I bent over in a belly laugh and tried to catch my breath. I stood back up and waved my hands in front of me to stop as

Bobby Ray continued to say funny things and twirl around like he was on ice skates.

Both of us fell onto his couch, laughing so hard our sides hurt.

"I don't know. He really did help me uncover some things I heard when I was at the emergency room." I turned my head against the couch cushion to find a horrid look on Bobby Ray's face. "Oh, don't worry. It was nothing you told me about how much you love me and can't ever imagine life without me."

"Mm-hmm, I said something like that."

I wasn't going to tell Bobby Ray about some of the things in the past I was starting to remember because I wasn't even sure myself what it was about. There were no reasons to recall any of it to Bobby Ray when I wouldn't be able to answer his questions.

"Where is it?" I asked. "When can we go get it?"

"I'd never believe you're in your thirties now."

"I'm not *in* my thirties." I exaggerated 'in.' "I am thirty."

"Mm-hmm, you're acting like a kiddo waiting for Santa to come down the pellet stove chimney," he joked. "Well, if there was a chimney." He referred to the pellet stove not having a chimney.

"It is almost Christmas. Which reminds me, I think it would be nice for you to show up tomorrow night at the Normal Baptist Church for the final Winter Festival choir event." I wanted Betts to have as much support as possible. "I know Betts would appreciate it."

"Fine."

"Fine!" I jumped around to face him on the couch, a little surprised he'd agreed so fast. "You're going?"

"Yeah." He rolled his eyes again.

"You do love me. You are so glad I'm not dead. I like this new attitude." I got to my feet and patted my leg to get Fifi up from the blanket on the floor, which was in front of the pellet stove.

"Your car is parked in front of my truck. You can drive it tomorrow after your doctor's appointment. Got it?" He wanted me to promise.

"Promise." I crossed my heart with my finger.

"Act your age." He smirked. "I hope you like it."

"I already love it." I zipped up my coat, and with Fifi next to me, I headed out the door. "Well, that wasn't too hard, to get him to come tomorrow night," I told Fifi and looked at the car he'd bought.

It was a simple four-door. A little bigger than the car I wrecked. But any car was fine with me. I'd hold true to my word and try not to sneak and steal it.

I didn't have time anyways. It was almost time for Hank to pick me up for our date, and I wanted to change into something a little dressier than the Happy Trails Campground sweatshirt I currently had on.

Plus, a little makeup would go a long way.

CHAPTER EIGHTEEN

On the way back to my camper, I grabbed Chester from Hank's camper so he could go potty and eat with Fifi. I didn't want to waste any time before going out to the Red Barn Restaurant with Hank for supper. I was starving.

Chester and Fifi ran around for the ten minutes that it took me to shower. They were waiting by the door and darted straight to the dog bowls after I let them in. Quickly, I poured a little kibble into their bowls and freshened up their water.

"Oh," I snarled when I noticed the water was a little dingy. "Hmm." I poured it out into the little kitchen sink and opened the small pantry—so small, it only kept a jug of fresh water and a broom—to get the water and pour it into their bowls.

I'd gotten a water-filtration system for the camper. Since I was pretty much always hooked up to the site and rarely drove the camper off, I kept it connected to the septic system and the well-water supply. It only made sense that my filter had met its end.

"We are going to have to head down to the Feed-N-Seed tomorrow to get us a filter," I told Fifi, "on our way to your grooming appointment." I sighed, thinking just how cute she and Chester were going to be at tomorrow night's Normal Baptist Church choir performance.

Santa was going to be there, and I just knew Fifi and Chester wanted a photo with him. I laughed at the thought, even though I was totally going to do it.

While the pups enjoyed their supper, I got out a black pair of pants and a black turtleneck to wear under my red puff vest that I'd picked up at the Thrifty Nickle. The Red Barn tended to be a little chilly during the winter months, depending on where they sat us, and I wanted tonight to be perfect.

The date was supposed to have happened the night of my wreck, so tonight was going to have to make up for it, and I couldn't wait.

I hadn't washed my hair in the shower because I couldn't really dry it with a blow-dryer. My curls would spring out and take up two chairs at the supper table. I put some gel in my hands and vigorously rubbed my palms together to evenly distribute the sticky stuff. I gently scrunched my curls with the gel, which would tame any unforeseeable springs from popping out.

"Now for a little makeup." I sighed and reached under the sink in the bathroom to get my makeup bag.

Boy, had my makeup changed. Long gone were the days of the big makeup stores I used to buy all my expensive products from. Now I went down to the local Piggly Wiggly and bought my namesake down in aisle twelve, Maybelline.

I laughed at the thought of my mama telling me how I'd gotten my name.

I remembered it as clear as day. We'd gone to the local dollar store, and Mama had told me she and daddy were going to go on a special night out. I was to watch my siblings. I recalled getting a little nervous about it because I was like nine or something. I couldn't believe they were going to let me babysit.

She'd taken me to the makeup section and picked the reddest lipstick she could find. When I had looked at the package, my name was written at the top.

Maybelline.

"*Mama, that's my name.*" My insides jumped at the white lettering that shone as bold as the sun.

"*That's right. When I found out I was pregnant with you. . .*" She took her hand and tucked a strand of my curls behind my ear.

I closed my eyes. I could still feel her fingernail trace the back of my ear. I could still smell the perfume she wore.

"*I was at the doctor's office. I walked out with a big smile on my face, and I couldn't wait to get to the coal mine to tell your daddy.*" Mama had the biggest and brightest smile. She always reminded me of an angel when she looked at me. "*There was a grocery mart near the mine, and I'd been in there several times to get your daddy a Coca-Cola when I'd go visit. That day, instead of getting Coco-Cola, I saw the makeup and knew I had to have the perfect shade of red on my lips as the words he'd been dying to hear came from my mouth.*"

Her sweet voice rang out like she was sitting in the bathroom with me. I sucked in a deep breath as I recalled the rest of mama's story.

"*Maybelline was the only one with the brightest red color.*" She showed me the package. "*'Maybelline,' I said to myself. That will be my baby's name. She's going to be too beautiful inside and out.*" Mama patted my head. "*And tonight, my sweet Maybelline is going to help mama out.*"

"Hello, honey, I'm home!" Hank laughed and broke me from my memory. "Mae?"

"Getting ready." I peeked my head out of the bathroom door. "Do you need to get changed?" I went back to throwing on a little makeup and took out the red lipstick I'd found at the Piggly Wiggly for this date.

"I already did. I went to let Chester out, and when he wasn't there, I knew you had him." Hank's footsteps came closer to the bathroom. "Wow, you look great." There was a fire in his eyes when he looked at me that made my heart go pitter-patter. It reminded me of how my dad had looked at my mom.

"Thank you." I picked up the red Maybelline lipstick. "New lipstick I'd picked up before the wreck."

"Love it." He bent down and kissed me. "Love you."

"I love you too." I slipped the lipstick into his jean pocket so he could carry it for me. "Ready? I'm starving." I followed him down the small hallway.

"I think my water filter needs to be replaced. I'll need to go to the Feed-N-Seed tomorrow." I grabbed my purse so I could get my cell phone since I didn't like to take my purse everywhere. "Did I tell you—" My voice cut off when my purse contents dumped all over the floor. "Ugh."

"Did you tell me what?" he asked as we both bent down to pick up all the junk. "That you are still looking into Randy's murder?" He picked up the notebook and waved it in the air before standing. He opened it and shook his head.

"No wonder Raye begged me to wait to transfer her." He sat down on the couch and flipped through the notes. "She said she clocked out and then went back in?"

"Okay. Hear me out." I put my hands out in front of him so he'd stay calm. "Christine Watson catered the Sinking Creek Winery. She has all sorts of information. But the main thing you need to know is that Denise had passed out from drinking too much, and this is the woman that came into my ER room to apologize. She's the one I overheard talking to Abraham about killing Randy."

"Whoa, whoa, Detective West." Hank had that smirk on his face that made me want to smack it right off him. "Who is Abraham, and how do you know this is the woman? Did you talk to her?"

"Well, no. Duh, I don't have a car. I didn't have a car until Bobby Ray gave me one." I shook my head to prevent Hank from asking me about it so we could stay on target. I had a point to get across. "Anyways, Tex had Meadow draw the woman I saw in my Reiki dream."

Slowly, Hank eased back, crossed one leg over the knee of his other leg, then folded his arms over his broad chest. His green eyes dulled, and his jaw tensed.

The awkward pause.

"You—"

"I—" We both talked at the same time.

"You go first." His voice was stern.

"No. You." I couldn't get a good read on his body language. It told me he was shutting me out, but his words encouraged me to keep talking. So I did. I proceeded with caution. "Fine. Yes. I went to see if Tex could unlock anything I'd overheard while I was knocked out in the ER. You said you told me all sorts of stuff, and well, everyone has asked if I remembered them talking to me while I was unconscious, so why not see if I could remember if I heard anyone killing Randy Lenz? I did." I tapped the sketch he'd found folded up in the notebook. "I overheard her and what I think to be the company lawyer, Abraham something-or-other." Currently, my mind wasn't cooperating with me on the actual last name, but it didn't matter at this point, so I continued to vomit the information I had.

"After I had this sketch done, I went to the library to research the company, and I had no idea it was a winery." I veered a little off course, but Hank's twitching eyebrow got me back on the subject at hand. "I remember Raye telling me how she and Denise were friends, so I took the sketch over there, and she told me all about Georgia Gammon and Randy Lenz's affair."

Hank sat there listening to me as I told the story and how I'd originally thought Denise had set up Georgia to kill her father.

"But she was passed out. I guess Georgia had to go to the hospital, but I'm not sure, but I have Ava looking into Randy Lenz's will to see if Georgia Gammon was supposed to take over the company."

Hank ran a hand through his thick hair.

"Where did the syringe go? Did you check out the video camera of the hospital?" I asked.

"Yes. And we've run it through the timeline, and honestly, according to Colonel, potassium is sudden death once it hits the veins. And Raye was gone for the second time before Randy Lenz took his last breath."

"Then she's innocent." I picked up the sketch. "I bet Georgia did it. But wait." My brows furrowed. "Why are you keeping Raye in jail?"

"I think if the killer knows we've arrested Raye for the crime, then they will become relaxed, and if this Georgia Gammon is or was supposed to somehow get a piece of the company, then maybe she'll start asserting her power, but we have a few other leads that I need to follow up on." He looked at the sketch again. "Even though I hate it, and I don't want you to be involved, there's no denying you did hear something. Would you be willing to go under a hypnosis?"

"What? Tex isn't good enough?" I asked.

"I'm just saying, sometimes the department uses a hypnosis technique to help crime victims remember things. I think a statement from you with a certified hypnosis would actually be more acceptable in my file."

"And bare-chested Tex who even ice-skates practically half-naked isn't acceptable?" I teased.

"Ice-skate?" Hank's head tilted, his mouth slightly open.

"We've got new guests." I stood up and put my hand out to help him up. "I'll tell you over supper."

"Oh, Mae." He sucked in a deep breath and stood up. He stared into my eyes. "What am I going to do with you?"

"You're gonna love me forever." I snuggled up to him.

"That's what I'm worried about." He gave me a light kiss on the top of my head.

Both of us told the four-legged babies goodbye before we headed out to Hank's truck, which was parked a few campsites down in front of his camper.

The snow had started to fall at a moderate pace.

"We are going to finish that Christmas tree," Hank reminded me when we passed by my camper in his truck. The little tree stood next to my camper with nary a bit of Christmas decoration on it.

"Sounds great." I smiled and caught a glimpse of my reflection in the window. There was a shock at the resemblance I had to my mother that I'd not recognized before. It had to be the bright-red lipstick.

"Do you really like my lipstick?" I had to break the tension between us.

"You're beautiful no matter what, with or without lipstick. But it does look good on you." He reached across the truck seat and put his hand on my leg.

I looked down and put my hand on his, intertwining our fingers. "My mom wore red lipstick only on special occasions," I said in almost a whisper, still afraid to talk about my past.

"I bet she wasn't as pretty as you." He was so sweet, trying to make me feel better.

"She was and is the prettiest lady I've ever seen." A faint smile crossed my face. "I remember being so excited as I watched my mom get ready for her date with my dad." I laughed. "Honestly, I should've known what was coming."

"What?" Hank asked, a passing car's headlights causing a shadow to pass over his face. "What was coming?"

"Their date. It was in the kitchen. They didn't have enough money to go out to eat, so my mom had me babysit my sister upstairs. But before my dad got home, I could see my mom was so excited. She'd put on her Sunday church dress, fixed her hair, and turned to me and asked if her lipstick looked good." I'd never forget how my mom nervously ran her hand down her hair and adjusted her dress when she heard Dad's car door shut. "He opened the door and took one look at my mom."

"And?" Hank was hanging on to every last word. He would glance at me then quickly turn his attention back to the road.

"She didn't need to say anything. He picked her up and swung her around." I looked away from Hank as the memory played in my head. "The red lipstick she had on was only worn when she had news that she was pregnant. I saw it one other time, and it was about a year before the fire." I gulped and looked back at Hank.

"I'm sorry. I thought it was going to be a good memory." He didn't need to apologize, but he was so sincere and heartfelt when it came to me.

"It is a good memory. And now you know how I got my name. Maybelline." Whenever I said my full name, I could hear it in my mom's voice.

"That's a good memory." He was right. "That's one you can recall over and over when you have those bad ones."

"Speaking of bad ones." I wasn't sure how much detail I wanted to get into, but the more I talked about my mom, the more I recalled the fire. "I also had a memory about the night of the fire."

"Yeah?" He slowly took the right turn into the parking lot of the Red Barn Restaurant. "Do you want to talk about it?"

The Red Barn used to be a hayloft at one time. The doors leading into the restaurant were refurbished old farm doors, which were completely insulated for the sake of it being converted from an old hayloft barn and horse stables to the restaurant.

The live garland was nice and thick with twinkling white Christmas lights scattered around it, giving it that old-time Christmas feel you'd see in movies. Nothing was better than the real thing.

"Let's go in and have a drink." It was Hank's way of not knowing how to deal with my sudden onset of emotions at this time.

I could feel my heart starting from anxiety. There was a distinct difference between an anxiety-driven beating heart and an excited drum. This one was definitely going all the way down my body and to my toes.

The short walk inside of the Red Barn was lost in my head. I did this a lot when I was driving. I'd get in the car and think about something that made me get lost in my thoughts, and before I knew it, I was at my destination. The same thing happened here.

If you'd told me before that an old farm barn could be romantic, I would have laughed and told you about some really neat place in New York City that'd charm the pants right off you when you stepped inside, but this old barn was so charming, and during Christmas, it was double the charm.

There were tall Christmas trees all along the walls. If I had to guess, I'd say there were at least ten in total. Since they'd kept as high a ceiling as they could, the trees were huge and decorated in various colors.

Long gone were the old stalls, haylofts, and dirt floor. The inside was completely open with exposed wooden beams. Each ceiling beam had strands of small and round light bulbs, which were bright enough so you could see what you were eating but were dimmed to induce the feeling as if you were under the moon. They'd gone as far as to dangle fake snowflakes from the beams, and it truly looked like a winter wonderland.

Tables draped with white linen cloths were scattered around, and the lanterns with the red candles at each table had been replaced with small ceramic Christmas trees that gave off just enough light to make it romantic.

I sucked in a deep breath as the hostess seated us. I made sure to look at the long bar in the back as we passed it to help get my mind off this anxiety beast that was on the edge of my nerves, just waiting for the opportunity to be released.

On the way to our table, I noticed the stage that was to the right of the bar. The band members were all dressed as Santa, and their jazz tunes were Christmas related.

"We will have a bottle of the house red wine." Hank gave the hostess the wine menu and sent her on her way. His green eyes sparkled when he looked at me, and I could tell he was trying to see if I'd gotten over whatever it was I was thinking over in the car.

No chance. It was on my mind, and I needed to tell him.

"I'm not sure, but I remember I was carried out of my family's house in the middle of the night in my nightdress." I gulped. The sudden rush of my heartbeat rang in my ears. My chest heaved up and down. The onset of a panic attack lingered along the edge of my mind. My nostrils flared as I looked out the window and told myself the things to be true.

"The color of your hair was black. The snow was white. The sky was dark. The red barn is red." The words flooded the silence between us. "The band is dressed up like Santa."

"What's going on?" Hank's voice cracked. He didn't seem to care if anyone noticed. He simply scooted his chair around the table to sit by me. He wrapped his arm around the back of my chair, gently rubbing the back of my arm.

"I am on the verge of a panic attack. I had them as a little girl. Mary Elizabeth took me to a therapist, and the therapist told me when I felt one coming that I needed to name tangible items."

Hank snuggled closer to me as though he were protecting me from any demons lurking inside of me.

"I'll Be Home for Christmas" was the band's next song. The drummer lightly tapped the wire brushes on the drums.

"I remember someone telling me to wait there for my parents. I can still feel the bottom of my nightdress brushing across my shins from the breeze that night. Then—" I let out a long breath through my mouth. I could feel his stare. "The house went up in flames." I turned my head to look at him. The picture was clear as day.

"Hank, I think someone caused the house fire on purpose."

Hank's eyes widened.

"I was spared. But why?"

CHAPTER NINETEEN

No matter how many times I replayed the new and vivid memory of someone physically carrying me outside where I knew for sure that someone had deliberately killed my family, I wasn't going to be able to solve it sitting around thinking about it.

Maybe there wasn't time to truly explore the past now. I did text my high school best friend, Jami Burkfield Mackenzie, though. It wasn't like we were super close anymore, but she still lived in Perrysburg, and she was married to Hunter Mackenzie, the mayor there and the brother of our mayor in Normal.

Jami had a prominent family, and her family owned the coal mine. Well, they practically owned Perrysburg. So if anyone could help me gather some answers, it'd be the Burkfield family.

My text simply told her that I hoped they had a Merry Christmas, and after the holidays I'd love to visit because I felt it was time to look into my family's house fire.

I didn't expect to hear back from her anytime soon.

Hank had also assured me that he would start looking into things but informed me that back then, records weren't kept like they were nowadays, even though both of us were in Perrysburg when the Fire Marshall came in and said he recalled the fire that night.

Maybe he was a start.

Though I hated to admit it, the thought of keeping my mind occupied with Randy Lenz's murder did help. And with Hank listening to my theory and what the Laundry Club ladies and I were planning this morning, he seemed to be open to anything we could figure out.

I smiled when I recalled what he'd said last night when he stopped by my camper to get Chester after our date, which was magical after I had my little panic attack.

"I don't get it, Mae. People just open up to you. Maybe you can get some information, but don't put yourself in danger." I swear my heart swelled when he followed up by saying, *"I almost lost you once this week. Don't do that to my heart again."*

"He does love me." I wiggled my shoulders and brought my coffee cup to my lips. Fifi danced around like she knew what I was saying. "Let's go over the clues one more time."

Fifi jumped up on the small couch and tucked herself in the bend of my legs to lay on top of the cream-colored Sherpa blanket.

With one hand gripping the mug, I opened the notebook and sat it in my lap, flipping through the clues Abby had written down about Randy Lenz.

"We've come to the conclusion that Denise didn't do it." I scanned the time frame of Denise's actions from the party and what Christine had said about Denise passing out, which led back to Abraham, who Denise ID'd as the man who carried her out of the party. "Then we have Abraham."

Over the rim of my coffee cup, I read everything Abby had written about him while I drank some more of my morning joy.

He was the lawyer for the winery, which meant he knew the guts of the operation, including the will. But if he and Georgia were in on the murder, why wouldn't he tell her about Randy changing the will? Or did Randy do it without Abraham knowing?

Those were some very good questions that we needed to find out when we went to the winery this morning.

"Come in," I hollered toward the camper door when someone knocked.

"Rise and shine." Queenie popped her head in. "It's time to get our dance on." She walked in with a stack of brightly colored spandex clothes that put a deep fear in me.

"Oh goodness." I groaned and uncurled my legs. Fifi jumped down off the couch and went to smell Queenie. "I hope I don't have to wear these for long."

"Just long enough to get into the winery, get what we need, and get out." She handed me the clothes. "Everyone is waiting. Stop this dilly-dallying and get dressed."

I turned to walk down the hallway when she stopped me.

"Don't worry about that messy hair of yours. Here."

I looked back to see what she wanted to give me.

"It's your very own Christmas headband. I've got a Christmas dance mix that'll knock your socks off." She pushed her headband up beyond her forehead. "Speaking of socks." She lifted her chin. "I gave you the pair that has bells." She picked up her foot and shook it, and jingling bells filled the air, making Fifi bark.

Normally, I would've protested. Actually, I wouldn't even have agreed to such an exercise, but this wasn't any normal situation. Truly, nothing was ever normal in Normal.

Instead of complaining and bemoaning, I walked to my bedroom and changed out of my comfortable clothes only to peel on the spandex.

There was a pause when I stared at myself in the mirror.

"Yep." I sighed. "Mary Elizabeth is right. Two things tell the truth: children and spandex." I ran my hand along my figure that was a lot fuller than when I'd come to Normal. "You'd think with all the hikes and trails I'd be in much better shape."

"Jazzercise will get you in shape." Queenie's big ears must've heard me. "Let's go!"

She darted out the door, and I made sure Fifi was good to go for the day since Dottie was going to be with me and wouldn't be able to come check on her. I would've asked Henry to let her out, but he was busy keeping an eye on the office while Dottie and I were gone.

"Good morning, everyone," I greeted Abby, Betts, Dottie, and Queenie when I opened the slider door of the cleaning van.

"Dottie, did you happen to tell Henry to keep an eye on the place this morning?" I didn't like to leave the campground without someone keeping an eye out.

Most campgrounds had a gate entrance with an office building right there, so any visitors or unexpected guests had to check in before they could enter. Happy Trails was so old that there wasn't any sort of entrance like that, so we had to make do, and today, that meant Henry.

"I sure did, but it didn't come without some fussing. That man has it better than any man I've ever seen," Dottie snarled from the front.

"At least he's going to." I eased down on the portable chair next to one of the vacuum cleaners. I was sure all the folding chairs Abby, Queenie, and I were sitting in weren't legal, but it was the best way we could all get around.

There was a lot of normal chitchat between the Laundry Club ladies. Most of it didn't pertain to anything other than a little bit of gossip here and there about the Winter Festival.

"I'm telling you, y'all are going to love it." Betts was so proud of the Normal Baptist Church's presentation tonight. "Bring your dogs, Mae."

"Oh, I am. I can't wait until you see Fifi's cute Christmas sweater." It was exciting.

"Okay, so what's the game plan?" Betts had already pulled into the driveway of the winery and stopped before she drove up into the parking lot.

"I figured we'd go inside the office building, which is different than their actual store where they give tours, wine tastings, and all the other junk they sell." Queenie had a plan, and I loved it. "I can go in and see the receptionist and tell her we are here for the final demonstration so they can put the final touches on next year's wellness plan."

"That's great," I gushed, happy to see she'd put some thought into it.

"Honey, there's more to this"—she shimmied her hands down her waist—"than just a fit body." She pointed to her brains.

We all laughed, and Betts threw the van back in drive.

Sinking Creek Winery appeared to have gotten its name from the deep creek bed that ran along the property. The grapevines extended as far as the eye could see and over the rolling hills. The snow had covered most of them, but I bet it was beautiful during the growing season. It was funny how Kentucky was known for bluegrass and limestone, both of which helped with feeding the right nutrients to build strong horses, but who knew how those two combinations helped to make some of the world's best wine?

"Right over there is the office building." Queenie directed Betts with her finger that she'd shoved past the front seats, gesturing out the windshield.

"We look like a bunch of yahoos from the eighties." Dottie's nose turned up.

I looked at Betts, who had on the hunter-green spandex outfit with a glittery Christmas tree on it. Betts stared at Abby, who wore a bright-red spandex unitard with a big Rudolph head on the front and had the notebook tucked under her arm. She glanced over at Dottie in her gold spandex outfit and a huge beaded yellow star square in the middle of her chest.

"Lordy-bee," Dottie grumbled. "We look like someone threw up Christmas."

"Oh, stop it. It's fun." Queenie led the pack of us up to the door. "Dancing is fun." She turned around, and before we entered, she said, "Now put a jolly, happy smile on your faces so they think y'all love Jazzercise."

Each one of us smiled so big the skin on our neck drew back. We tumbled through the doors, laughing at one another.

"Well, if this isn't what we need around here." The woman behind the desk had short brown hair that waved down to the middle of her ears.

"I'm sorry." Queenie did this chancy move up to the desk. "Did my dancers and I come at a bad time?" She looked at her wrist as if she had a watch on. She didn't. "I have an appointment for the final demonstration with the board executives for the finishing touches of the upcoming yearly wellness program," she lied. "Is Randy in?" She went in for the stab. "Loosen up, ladies," she snapped at us.

I started to roll my head around my neck. Dottie threw out her leg a couple of times in what looked like a rag doll move. Abby did a few punches in the air, and Betts busted into jumping jacks.

None of us did any sort of dance moves.

"Oh, Mr. Lenz. . ." The woman teared up. "He was looking forward to your demonstration today, but—" The woman pulled in her lips. She glanced left and then right. "He died. He was murdered," she whispered.

"Murdered?" all of us said out loud. At least it sounded better than our loosening-up Jazzercise skills looked. Or at least, it did seem a little more convincing.

"Shh." The woman put her finger up to her mouth. "Everyone is a mess. The board is meeting right now about it."

"In there?" I pointed to a room behind her and looked past her through the glass door, where I saw Ava Cox. "There's Ava."

"Ma'am, ma'am." The receptionist stood up and tried to meet me before I hurried past her. "You can't go in there. They aren't going to do Jazzercise with you."

"Good morning!" I burst through the door with my arms spread wide open.

"Mae?" Ava's jaw dropped to the ground. "What are you dressed like that, and why are you here?" she asked through a huge smile, attempting to cover up her obvious confusion.

"You." Dottie rushed in behind me. The winter sun shined through the window and hit Dottie's golden star just right, sending all sorts of little light flecks around the boardroom. "Are you Georgia Gammon?"

Dottie looked at Abby and snapped her fingers. It was like they had this unspoken language between them.

Abby opened the notebook and took out the sketch Meadow had done.

"Yep. I'd say that's her." Abby looked at it and handed it to Dottie. "This here is the killer."

"Killer?" Georgia planted her hands on the conference table. She hit a button on the phone in front of her. The receptionist answered on speakerphone. "Please call the sheriff." Georgia Gammon's eyes blazed with anger as she stared at me across the table, where about fifteen board members sat, all eyes on me.

Suddenly, I was very aware of the inappropriate action I'd just taken by busting through the door.

"Excuse me," Ava said with a cheerful voice and grabbed me with one hand and Dottie with the other. "Outside, ladies," she muttered through gritted teeth.

"You don't understand." Betts was trying to get her voice heard on the way out of the conference room. "Raye Porter didn't kill Randy Lenz, nor did Denise Lenz."

"Wait. A. Minute." A young lady in a blue pantsuit with honey-blond hair parted to the side walked out with Ava. "I didn't kill my father, if that's what you're insinuating."

"I said you didn't," Betts corrected Denise. "We are here because we wanted to look into your father because Mae—" Queenie pushed me from behind, sending me nose-to-nose with Denise. "Mae heard Georgia and Abraham plotting to kill your dad."

"This is ridiculous. We didn't kill anyone." Georgia appeared, and the man I'd seen with her at my ER room stood beside her.

"You were going to." I changed my focus from Denise to Georgia. "You two saw the syringe, and I heard you"—I pointed to Abraham—"tell her to shoot him with the syringe. Granted, Georgia didn't want to, and she said that he probably wasn't going to make it anyways, but you told her that she needed to make sure and to kill him."

Abraham's mouth opened and closed a few times before Sheriff Jerry Truman bolted through the door.

CHAPTER TWENTY

"That didn't go so well." The five of us had tucked tail after Jerry gave us a good talking-to, and we found ourselves back in the van. "But they did take in Georgia and Abraham for questioning." I felt almost sick to my stomach.

"Hank didn't sound too happy on the phone." Abby shot me a withering glance. "I bet he didn't look happy either."

"I'm just glad he didn't show up." Betts's voice cracked. She was almost in tears when Jerry told her how he should arrest us for putting fear into the other board members.

"But he didn't say we didn't have some valid clues." Queenie made a great point.

"I just don't trust that Ava." Dottie unsnapped the cigarette case and tapped out a smoke. She rested it between her fingers, unlit of course. I guessed holding it was something that made her feel better. "Do you reckon she was telling the truth about seeing the will?"

"When I asked Ava this morning to look up the will, she was doing what we all agreed on." Betts did say she would contact Ava about it. "You just busted through the door before she could get down to the nitty-gritty."

"Yeah." I gnawed on my cheek and wondered what Hank was going to say. "I wish I hadn't busted in."

"Honey, you've got a concussion." Queenie patted my spandex leg.

Betts was driving the van as fast as she could to get me to my appointment with Dr. Mel. We'd never figured on having the law called on us and being held against our will.

"I feel fine, and I hope Dr. Mel tells me I'm good in a few minutes." I appreciated her kind words, but there was no excuse for my behavior.

"Well, tell everyone it was your concussion." Queenie winked. "That way, we won't all look stupid."

"We do look stupid in these outfits." Dottie wasn't about to let that comment slide by.

Everyone in the car started to bicker and banter about the outfits to the unruly behavior each one of us was ashamed about.

I could hear Hank now talking about me and the Laundry Club ladies: *"You five are not good for anyone. I told you to look into some things, not all of you."*

"Stop!" I screamed into the van. "Y'all are hurting my concussion."

Queenie jerked her head toward me, smiled, and winked. She knew I was lying just to get them to be quiet.

"Now. I'm going to go into that hospital and go to my appointment. All y'all stay put. You look utterly ridiculous in those outfits and might make someone sicker than they are." I got out of the folding chair and walked, hunched over, to the sliding door and hobbled out. "Ridiculous. I can't take y'all nowhere." A little bit of Mary Elizabeth came out of me. I smiled. She would get a kick out of seeing all of us in these crazy spandex outfits.

The stares, snickers, and giggles didn't go unnoticed when I passed by people in the hospital. If I'd had the courage, I'd have belted out a Christmas tune as if I were delivering a Christmas gram.

"Oh my." Pamela eyeballed me as I walked through the hallway on my way to the doctors' building. "Mae? Has your concussion gotten worse?"

For a split second, I was stunned, wondering why she'd think such a thing.

"The outfit." I threw my head back. "Actually, I'm so glad to see you. Do you remember the man who died next to me when I was in the ER?" I asked only because she was my nurse on that shift, and it was Raye who had been there.

"Randy Lenz." Her eyes grew. "That's a whole mess. That's why I'm here. Raye Porter lost her job, and she'd just gotten the nurse manager job for day shift, so they needed me to fill in."

"They fired her?" My jaw dropped, and we took two steps to the side to let people pass us.

"Oh yeah. She was arrested, but they let her go this morning." Pamela frowned. "Shame too. She is a great nurse practitioner."

"If Hank let her go, then why was she fired?" I asked.

"Hank?" Pamela's face lit up. Her phone buzzed in the pocket of her scrubs. She took it out. "That's right. You and he are married." She looked at her phone.

"We aren't married," I rushed to say. "We are dating." I peeked down at the screen.

Two little kids popped up as the phone's screen saver.

"My babysitter. I need to take this. Sorry." She moved past me to hurry off. "It was good seeing you." She waved and smiled over her shoulder before she put the phone up to her ear. "Hello."

It was good to know Hank had let Raye go, but it sure didn't fit with his theory that if there was a real killer out there, then Raye would be the pawn. I shook the thought out of my head because right now, I was there to get the all clear so I could get in my new car and do my own thing without these crazy spandex pants on.

"Whoa! Look at those pants." Preston was pushing an empty gurney through the hall and nearly ran me over. He stopped. "Mae. Right?"

"Yeah. Preston." I couldn't help but smile at the young man.

"Goodness, I'd never figure you for that type of outfit, which is fine." He seemed a bit confused. "Anyways, was that Pamela I saw you talking to?"

"It was. She was telling me about Raye Porter losing her job." I could see a little switch flip on in his head. "I can't believe she'd get fired over being falsely accused of murder." I pulled out my phone to check the time. If I didn't hurry, I was going to be late.

"She didn't get fired for that. She got fired because she took it upon herself to go against hospital rules, ordering the patient's medication for a procedure that hadn't happened. Plus, she's not even a nurse on that floor." He shook his head. "I like Raye, and I think she'd be much easier to work for than Pamela, since she was the only other nurse who applied for the nurse manager job. It is good for her because now she won't lose her kids in that bitter custody battle."

"Pamela?" I questioned.

"Yep." Pamela passed by in a rush then abruptly stopped. "Did y'all just say my name?"

"I was just telling Mae how you got the new head-nurse manager position." Preston put his hands back on the gurney. "Gotta go get a patient from X-ray. Good seeing you, Mae."

"Where are you headed?" Pamela asked me.

"I was going to grab a coffee before I head to my doctor's appointment with Dr. Mel." I had some questions for Pamela to answer now that she might be aware of all the comings and goings of the Lenz family and lawyer. "You got a minute?"

She looked at her watch and pondered for a second. "Sure." She shrugged. "Why not? I don't have to rush around since I'm in charge. Let's get a coffee from the employee room."

"That's great. Both are great. Coffee with you and you getting the job." I walked next to her, letting her lead as I moved out of the way of oncoming people. "This place is busy."

"It's always busy." She laughed. "I'm not sure if I can get used to this day-shift thing after being on night shift for so long, but I'm willing to give it a shot."

We had some chitchat while waiting for the elevator up to the ER floor. I would just have to be late.

"My boyfriend, Hank—you know, the detective—has a couple of

people in custody. I wanted to know if you had any remembrance of Rand Lenz's girlfriend and lawyer coming that night." It was a long shot, but any clues would help. "I think I overheard them talking about the syringe."

"Really?" Pamela's eyes grew. "Unbelievable. You know your boyfriend was in here this morning going over the videotapes and the comings and goings of the nursing staff that night, and I wonder if it was about them?"

"Do you believe in Reiki?" I asked since it was such a strange thing to talk about, and I already looked like more of a fool in this outfit.

"I don't even know what that is." She snickered.

"It's a form of holistic medicine." I followed her into the coffee room where we'd gone the morning I'd overheard Raye and Dr. Mel arguing.

"Oh, we don't really do holistic medicine here." She shook her head.

"I wasn't saying here. I had it done through a friend." I didn't bother going into great detail about it. "But it sometimes helps recall memories. And I have to tell you that I remember Randy's lawyer and girlfriend discussing killing him with a syringe before I heard Raye come in there."

"I'd believe it." She nodded. "I've never met anyone in my short career who has, but they tell us in nursing school that it's believed people in comas can hear what's going on around them. This Reiki helped you?" Pamela grabbed the hot coffee carafe, and I retrieved two Styrofoam cups from the stack.

"I was able to recall what the girlfriend looked like and got a sketch. Dead on her. I also recalled Raye going in there and looking for the syringe. But it was gone." I held the cups, and she poured. "Ouch." I dropped one of the coffees.

Pamela had overpoured the coffee and nearly burnt my skin off.

"Oh my gosh!" She put the pot down. "I'm so sorry. I was listening to your story and just wasn't paying attention. Here." She took the other cup from me, and I bent over in pain, holding my hand to my stomach.

"You stay right there, and I'll go grab something. Oh my goodness," I heard her muttering as she hurried out the door.

It seemed like it was taking her a long time, so I ran to the bathroom where she'd excused herself the morning I was being discharged and ran my hand under cold water.

It felt like my hand was on fire. My mind circled back to the heat that I had felt standing in the front yard of my childhood home. The memory flooded back to me as I watched the water flow over my beet-red hand.

"If you think I'm going to let you take custody of my kids, you've got another thing coming to you." There was a hushed whisper coming from behind the curtain. *"I swear, I don't know how I'll do it, but I'll kill you before I let you take my kids from me."*

"Mae, are you in there?" The door flew open, and Pamela rushed in. "I'm so sorry. Let me see it."

I pulled my hand out from underneath the water.

"You're shaking." She took my hand. "I can't believe I did this," she whispered and put some sort of ointment on it.

I gulped. Her whisper sounded eerily familiar.

"I'm sorry. I need to check on Mr. Lenz. Can you step outside for just a second?" The woman's voice sounded just like Pamela.

"Sure," Georgia Gammon agreed. *"Lawrence and I'll be right out here."*

"You can head down to the nurses' station and get a coffee if you like," Pamela suggested. *"I'll only be a second."*

My hand suddenly stopped hurting, and I pulled it away from hers.

"Are you in pain?" Pamela's brows pinched. "I'm so sorry."

"Did you say you had kids?" I asked and focused on her body language.

"I do." She smiled. Her eyes narrowed.

"Aren't you in a bitter custody battle?" I asked. "Something about childcare." I was saying things out loud that didn't make any sense to me.

It was just like Tex had said: some things might come back to me a little at a time or. . .something about a puzzle.

"Memories will come like pieces of a puzzle," I whispered.

147

"I'm going to grab one more thing for you to put on it." Pamela turned and headed out of the bathroom. "I'll be right back."

My mind was racing. I looked down at my hand and winced at the throbbing pain from the burn.

"Pamela is in a bitter custody battle with her ex. He is going to get custody because she can't care for them because she works night shift." The memory pieces of my knowledge of Pamela started to come to me, just like Tex had mentioned. "None of Randy's family or friends killed him."

My heart jumped.

"I've got to get out of here." I swung open the bathroom door and rushed across the room, only to be met by Pamela on the other side of the door.

"Hey. Where ya going?" Pamela questioned with a cheery tone. "I think you should get a little shot of morphine for that hand of yours." She walked into the room.

I took a couple of steps backwards.

She pulled a syringe from her pocket. "This might be a little too much. You'll love the high that you'll get, but unfortunately, you'll have overdosed." She smiled. "We see it here all the time. Patients come in here and need pain medication because most of them get hooked on painkillers after, say. . .a car wreck."

"Hold on. Are you saying that you're going to kill me like you killed Randy Lenz?" I held my hands up in front of me. "I mean, I knew you needed to move shifts, but to kill a man so Raye could get fired, leaving the door open for you? Now that you have your job, Preston is right—you won't lose your kids." My jaw dropped, and my eyes widened. "Wow, a mother's love is endless. Even at the expense of an innocent man's life."

"You don't have kids. You have no idea what it's like to carry a child, much less two." Pamela put a hand to her forehead and rubbed it. Shaking her head, she glanced up at me. "I carried them in my body. Now, because I'm trying to make a good living, I'm getting punished for having a job at night. He's suing me for full custody, and my lawyer said he was going to get it because I work nights."

"They can't do that." I was going to say anything to get Pamela to move away from the door so I could run out.

"Oh, they were, but I had to keep my kids safe. You have to understand that, Mae. Or do you?" Her eyes narrowed and hardened. She flipped the lid off the syringe and held the needle point to the light. She used her other hand to flick it a couple of times then pushed the plunger just enough for a trickle of whatever was in there to dribble out.

"I don't need any morphine. I'm fine." I kept my eye on her hands. "I didn't even fill the prescription Dr. Mel had given me when he discharged me."

"It's okay. I've got just the thing for you, and when they find you, we will all tell them how concussions really do mess up people's minds, as well as an addiction to morphine." There was unbridled anger in her voice with a hint of fear.

"Listen, I told you. I date Hank, and he can get you out of anything." I was starting to panic. There wasn't much room between me, her, and the door. If I made one wrong inch to either side, she could simply reach out and jab the syringe in me.

"I don't need your help. You do understand, though, why I had to frame Raye for it?" she questioned, like she needed me to know she was within her rights to take a man's life. "Mae, you are going to die today." Pamela's voice had become emotionless, and it chilled me to the bone.

As if in slow motion, Pamela took one step toward me while raising her arm with the syringe over her head. Her hand gripped the syringe, and her thumb automatically went on top of the plunger.

"I'm sorry it had to go this way." She took another step closer.

I took a step backwards and put my hands behind my back to see where I was going. My hands caught on the table, and immediately, my mind went to the coffee pot, the hot coffee in the coffee pot.

Looking out of the corner of my eye, I reached for it, and in one fluid motion, I gripped the coffee pot and flung the open end at Pamela, dousing her right in the face.

The awfullest noises of pain came out as she screamed. The syringe fell from her grip, and her hands covered her face as her knees buckled, and down to the ground she went.

As fast as I could, I ran around her and bolted out the door.

"Help! Help! Security!" I yelled when I made it out into the hallway.

CHAPTER TWENTY-ONE

"You mean to tell me that she killed Randy Lenz because she wanted on day shift?" Dottie still couldn't get over why Pamela had killed Randy, even though it'd been a few hours since the ordeal.

I couldn't tell if it was smoke rolling out of her mouth or her hot breath puffing into the freezing cold. Either way, she and the rest of the Laundry Club ladies were a little taken back when I came out of the hospital and told them I'd nearly just died from a morphine overdose from Randy Lenz's killer.

"Yep." I held Chester's leash in one hand and Fifi's in the other. "Hank is doing the transport papers now. He said he'd meet us here."

"There you are. I heard you were going to be here." Raye had found me in the crowd. "I wanted to thank you for helping me. Ava said you were amazing at these things. I know what I did was wrong in getting everything set up for Randy, but I love his family so much that I had to make sure he got the best care possible when he was to come out of open heart." She teared up. "I know I didn't go with policy, but sometimes I have to go with my heart."

"Are you going to be okay?" I asked.

"Yes. In fact, Denise is the rightful owner of the winery now. She is moving forward with her dad's vision to have a healthy workplace and did hire me as the nurse practitioner on site."

"That's wonderful." I gave her a great big Christmas hug. "You deserve it especially since the hospital didn't take you back."

"Well, it's like a Christmas miracle. It all worked out." Her smiled. "I've gotta run. I don't want to miss the singing."

I looked around, and when I saw Betts gathering all the choir members to go to the front steps of the Normal Baptist Church, I smiled. She seemed happy being in control of the event. Betts had been so involved in the church as the pastor's wife, and now that he was gone and she was an ex, she'd been a bit lost over the past couple of years. But with anything, time has seemed to heal up some of her wounds.

The choir wore thick red robes and blended in well with all the poinsettia plants strategically placed on each rung of the steps.

There were barrels of fires going along the front lawn of the church. The smell of kettle corn caught my attention, and I looked over to where Christine Watson was giving out cups of her Winter Festival Eggnog, non-alcoholic, I was sure.

"There's Abby," I told Dottie and lifted my chin up in the air with a smile on my face, hoping to catch Abby's attention since my hands were occupied with the leashes.

When Abby stopped in the crowd, I curled up on my toes to see who she was talking to because her smile was brighter than the Christmas star.

"I'm so sorry you're in here. Oh, May-bell-ine, please wake up. Please." Bobby Ray rubbed my hands. He put his head down on my hand. A tear dripped from his eyes onto my hand. He sat up and used his finger to rub his tear into my skin. "I wish I'd told you about me and Abby. I'm worried you'll never know. Oh, Mae, you'd be so happy to know that we've been dating a few weeks, and I swear I love her. May-bell-ine, please come back so we can tell you. I'm so sorry we kept it from you."

The crowd parted as my memory of Bobby Ray talking to me while I was unconscious in the hospital appeared.

Abby threw her arms around a man, and when he turned to kiss her,

EGGNOG, EXTORTION, & EVERGREENS

it was Bobby Ray. Only it was a clean-cut Bobby Ray. Even the back of his hair had been trimmed, and he had on a pair of jeans and a flannel shirt. Still the same work boots, but he had cleaned himself up rather nice.

"Oh my gosh." I gasped at the sight of them.

"What?" Dottie took a puff of her cigarette.

"Bobby Ray and Abby are dating." I blinked a few times to make sure what I was seeing was real.

"Oh yeah." Dottie's nose curled, and she shook her head. "They think they are all secretive-like. I see headlights coming up the drive of the campground. The car never goes by, so I started watching. I see her little ponytail swinging side to side when she runs up and tries not to be seen. But I seen her sneaking in his bungalow a time or two. Maybe five."

"Hey." Hank walked up behind me and wrapped his arms around me. "What are you two doing?" He took Chester's leash with one hand and mine with his other.

I squeezed Hank's hand and looked at him. He peered down at me with his big green eyes and smiled.

"We are looking at Normal's newest couple." Dottie sighed.

The crackle of a sound system got the attention of the crowd. The show was about to start. I turned my attention back to Betts. She had a microphone in her hand and was walking up to the front of the church with the choir in position so she could give her welcome speech.

"I love you," I whispered and laid my head on Hank's shoulders. My heart and soul were filled with love, with love to be alive, growing as the choir sang beautiful music, and filled with joy that Bobby Ray and Abby had found each other.

This year, Christmas delivered love in a big way to Happy Trails Campground, and I could only believe the next year was going to be Happy Trails Campground's best year yet.

My phone vibrated a text in the pocket of my heavy coat. I took it out.

I gulped.

It was Jami Burkfield Mackenzie.

Maybe all these crimes I'd been nosing around in was preparing me to solve the biggest mystery of my life.

What really happened to my family home?

THE END

If you enjoyed reading this book as much as I enjoyed writing it then be sure to return to the Amazon page and leave a review.

Go to Tonyakappes.com for a full reading order of my novels and while there join my newsletter. You can also find links to Facebook, Instagram and Goodreads.

Are you ready to head into the new year with Mae West and the Laundry Club ladies? Don't miss out on the all the fun. Continue your camping vacation in Normal, Kentucky, with Ropes, Riddles, & Robberies, book 15 in A Camper and Criminals Cozy Mystery. Keep reading for a sneak peek of Ropes, Riddles, & Robberies which is also available to purchase on Amazon or read for FREE in Kindle Unlimited.

BUT WAIT! Readers ask me how much my cozy mysteries and the characters in them reflect my real life. Well...here is a good story for you.

WHOOO HOOO!! I'm so glad we are a week out from last Coffee Chat with Tonya and happy to report the poison ivy is almost gone! But y'all we got more issues than Time magazine up in our family.

When y'all ask me if my real life ever creeps into books, well...grab your coffee because here is a prime example!

My sweet mom's birthday was over the weekend. Now, I'd already decided me and Rowena was going to stay there for a couple of extra days.

On her birthday, Sunday, Tracy and David were there too, and we were talking about what else...poison ivy! I was telling them how I can't stand not shaving my legs. Mom and Tracy told me they don't shave daily and I might've curled my nose a smidgen. And apparently it didn't go unnoticed.

I went inside the house to start cooking breakfast for everyone and mom went up to her room to get her bathing suit on and Tracy was with me. All the men were already outside on the porch.

The awfulest crash came from upstairs and my sister tore out of that kitchen like a bat out of hell and I kept flipping the bacon. My mom had fallen...shaving her legs!

Great. Now it's my fault.

Her wrist was a little stiff but she kept saying she was fine. We had a great day. We celebrated her birthday, swam, and had cake. When it came time for everyone to leave but me and Ro, I told mom that she should probably go get an x-ray because her wrist was a little swollen.

After a lot of coaxing, she agreed and I put my shoes on and told Tracy, David, and Eddy to go on home and we'd call them.

My mama looked me square in the face and said, "You're going with that top knot on your head?"

I said, "yes."

She sat back down in the chair and said, "I'm not going with you lookin' like that."

"Are you serious?" I asked.

"Yes. I'm dead serious. I'm not going with you looking like that. What if we see someone?" She was serious, y'all!

She protested against my hair!

Now...this is exactly like the southern mama's I write about! I looked at Eddy and he was laughing. Tracy and David were laughing and I said, "I can't wait until I tell my coffee chat people about this."

As you can see in the above photo, the before and after photo.

Yep...we went and she broke her wrist! Can you believe that? We were a tad bit shocked, and I'll probably be staying a few extra days (which will give us even more to talk about over coffee next week).

Oh...we didn't see anyone we knew so I could've worn my top knot! As I'm writing this, you can bet your bottom dollar my hair is pulled up in my top knot!

Okay, so y'all might be asking why I'm putting this little story in the back of my book, well, that's a darn tootin' good question.

This is exactly what you can expect when you sign up for my newsletter. There's always something going on in my life that I have to chat with y'all about each Tuesday on Coffee Chat with Tonya. Go to Tonyakappes.com and click on subscribe in the upper right corner to join.

Chapter One of Book Fifteen
Ropes, Riddles, & Robberies

There's always a good feeling when the calendar turns to a new year. The feeling of renewal, hope, change and just getting a do over. For me, Mae West, this year was going to be sort of a rebirth. A rebirth of who I had become and why I had become who I was.

Not that I didn't know who I was. I certainly knew that and I didn't have any control that my entire family had died in a house fire and I was clearly the one left to be spared.

Yes. I believed that I was spared.

How or why did I believe that was a whole 'nuther way of thinking and there was no harm done in trying to figure out if my recent memories of the house fire event unfolded was not an accident as the Fire Marshall had claimed it was and was deliberate, I was on a mission this year to find out.

One problem.

I didn't live there and this was over fifteen years ago when the fire had taken place. I had no idea if the people who lived in my hometown of Perrysburg, Kentucky was still alive or even around.

There was one person in particular that I did know who was around and that was Jami Burkfield Mackenzie. My school best friend. We'd been friends for a long time. It wasn't by chance we happened to pick each other as friends, my father made me be friends with her.

At the coal mine company picnic to be exact.

I remembered it like it was yesterday.

My mom had taken me and my sister to the local second hand store. She had thumbed through those racks with me hanging on her leg and my sister stuck on her hip. The sound of those steel hook hangers screeched as she shoved and pushed them aside to look at the next piece of clothing on the rack.

"This will be pretty for the picnic." I watched her pluck the red and white checkered dress off the rack. "Look up, Maybelline." She shoved the clothes hanger up under my chin as she held the dress up to me. "Step back, Maybelline. Why do you always have to be right on my leg, honey?"

Maybe because I was a little girl and wanted the comfort of being next to my mom? Was that really such a hard concept for her? Probably not and I never sassed back to her, I just stepped back and took the hanger so she could get a look for herself.

"Do you like it?" Her eyes glowed. "It makes your curls stand out and your beautiful skin," my mom sighed. "You're the best thing I ever made."

"No." My baby sister would giggle. "Sugar cookies are the best thing, mama."

Mom and I would laugh. Her laugh was so amazing. My mom was beautiful. She reminded me of a movie star with her long black eye lashes, her long black straight hair, and her olive skin. When she laughed, her mouth would open wide and end with a bright smile. My baby sister looked just like her.

Not me.

I looked just like my dad. He had nice and thick curly brown hair. He had deep hazel eyes that always looked like he was studying something or thinking on an important project. After all, he was the foreman for the local coal mine company. Which brought me right back to Jami Burkfield Mackenzie.

The Burkfield's owned the coal mine. Heck, they practically owned everything in and around Perrysburg, so it was only natural that half the town worked for them.

"Maybelline, you be nice to Jami Burkfield." My dad always made sure me and my little sister minded our p's and q's when we were around any of the Burkfield's.

The yearly company picnic in particular.

"She's my boss's granddaughter and she's your age. I'm sure you two would get along." I remember looking out the window when we pulled up to their big fancy house on the outskirts of town.

I'd never seen the likes.

They had an entire compound like the famous Kennedy family I'd seen my mom gawk at in those magazines while we were in line at the local grocery store. Mom would quickly thumb through them and read as much of the celebrity gossip she could.

One time the cashier had gotten on mom for bending the pages of the magazine and putting it back. Told mom not to pick them up if she wasn't going to buy it.

"They aren't there for you to look through and put back." The cashier glared at my mom. It was one of those glares where she had shifted her focus to me and my little sister with a snarled nose. Like she was better than us and we were just dirty kids from the wrong side of the track.

We weren't. We were clean and my mom made sure of it every time she took us to town.

"One day Maybelline," my mom told me when we'd get back in the car after the cashier got mad, "you're gonna be famous and on the front of these magazines." She pinch my chin and smile. "Then we won't have to read about famous people, because we will be the famous people."

That was my mom. She always had big dreams and big hopes.

After that day when we'd go to the grocery she'd look for that cashier and get in a different line. She still thumbed through the magazines.

But I did remember this story after my face was plastered on a few magazines in the grocery check-out. Granted, it was mainly the National Enquirer after my ex-now dead-husband Paul West had gotten caught for trying to pull off the biggest Ponzi scheme in the United States.

But the fire that killed my family haunted me to this day. I'd really ran from my childhood by climbing out the window of my foster mom's house the exact minute in the middle of the night I turned eighteen.

I had climbed on a greyhound bus and when we passed the Welcome To Perrysburg sign at the county line as we rolled out of town, I swore to myself I'd never be back in that town again.

Years later and after remembering a few key details about the night of the house fire that killed my family, I was planning my trip back to Perrysburg because I didn't believe the fire was an accident.

My family was murdered. I was going to prove it.

I hope you enjoyed your vacation in Normal, Kentucky that included a little southern hospitality with a smidgen of homicide. Continue the sleuthing fun with Ropes, Riddles, & Robberies, book 15 in A Camper & Criminals Cozy Mystery.

RECIPES AND CLEANING HACKS FROM MAE WEST AND THE
LAUNDRY CLUB LADIES AT THE HAPPY TRAILS CAMPGROUND
IN NORMAL KENTUCKY.

Slow Cooker 3 Bean Chili

The slow cooker is one of my favorite kitchen tools because using it makes it possible for me to prepare great meals that don't require me to actually be there when it is cooking. For most slow cooker meals, prep takes no longer than 5 to 10 minutes. Throw a few things together in the morning and come home to dinner that's hot and ready in a few hours. Short of having a personal chef, that's a pretty great deal.

I like to serve this chili with something on top like shredded cheese, creamy polenta, chopped onion, sour cream, or the time-honored way with just a handful of oyster crackers.

Ingredients

- ½ lb. 80/20 ground beef (or meat of choice or no meat.)
- 1 small yellow onion, diced
- 1 can pinto beans
- 1 can dark red kidney beans
- 1 can chili beans
- 1 large can crushed tomatoes
- 2 cups water
- 2 garlic cloves, minced
- 2 teaspoons cumin
- 2 teaspoons chili powder
- 2 teaspoons dried oregano
- Salt and pepper

Directions

1. Add ground beef and onion to a pan and cook over medium heat until meat is well browned. Drain fat and discard.

2. Transfer meat and onion to slow cooker, add remaining ingredients and stir to combine.
3. Cover and set heat to low. Cook on low setting for 6-8 hours.
4. Taste for seasoning, add salt and pepper to taste, and serve.

Hack on conserving your water supply

Use a dish pan in your sink. Yep!

Purchase a dish pan that will fit in the kitchen sink of your RV. When you finish doing the dishes consider "disposing" of the dishwater in one of four ways rather than sending it down the kitchen drain to the grey tank:

Where legal (most everywhere), use it to water a thirsty bush just like tent camping.

Use it to quench the evening campfire.

Dump it down the toilet into the black tank.

Save it in a gallon milk jug and use it to flush the toilet.

Perfect Toasted Cheese

Now what would a great bowl of soup be without a piping hot toasted cheese sandwich to eat with it? For a perfect toasted cheese sandwich, butter one side each of two slices of hearty whole wheat bread (or white if you must) and layer your favorite cheese in between. Cook your sandwich in a frying pan over medium high heat until the bread is golden and toasty and the cheese has begun to melt, about 3-4 minutes per side.

Grey Tank Hack

Do you know what the grey tank is for? It's for the sink water. I'm horrible when it comes to conserving sink water when I'm washing up the RV dishes. I've learned a little trick.

Spray your dishes before washing them.

Purchase a spray bottle and fill it with a mixture of dish soap, water, and a little vinegar. Spray the mixture on dirty dishes and wipe before washing which will greatly reduce the amount of water required to finish washing them.

Less water used equals less wastewater in the grey tank. Dawn dish soap is a favorite among many RVers.

Kentucky Eggnog

Ingredients

- 1 liter Bourbon Whiskey
- 1 quart milk
- 1 quart heavy cream
- 2 dozen eggs
- 1 1/2 cups sugar
- Nutmeg, garnish

Directions

1. Separate eggs and beat yolks until creamy.
2. Whip sugar into yolks.
3. Beat whites until they stand in peaks
4. Add 1/2 cup additional sugar, if desired.
5. Beat yolks and bourbon together
6. Add whites.
7. Beat cream.
8. Add cream and milk to mixture.
9. Add nutmeg to taste and garnish.

Camper Tip From Fifi

Don't change your dog's routine .

Dogs do best if their basic routine never changes If your dog's normal at-home routine looks like this:

Walk

Breakfast

Nap

Snack

Walk

Dinner

He will be happiest if he has the same basic routine when he is RV camping too. Bring his favorite bed from home as well as the same food and snacks.

A NOTE FROM TONYA

Thank y'all so much for this amazing journey we've been on with all the fun cozy mystery adventures! We've had so much fun and I can't wait to bring you a lot more of them. When I set out to write about them, I pulled from my experiences from camping, having a camper, and fond memories of camping.

Readers ask me if there's a real place like those in my books. Sadly, no. It's a combination of places I've stayed and would own if I could.
XOXO ~ Tonya

For a full reading order of Tonya Kappes's Novels, visit
Tonyakappes.com

BOOKS BY TONYA
SOUTHERN HOSPITALITY WITH A SMIDGEN OF HOMICIDE

Camper & Criminals Cozy Mystery Series

All is good in the camper-hood until a dead body shows up in the woods.

BEACHES, BUNGALOWS, AND BURGLARIES
DESERTS, DRIVING, & DERELICTS
FORESTS, FISHING, & FORGERY
CHRISTMAS, CRIMINALS, AND CAMPERS
MOTORHOMES, MAPS, & MURDER
CANYONS, CARAVANS, & CADAVERS
HITCHES, HIDEOUTS, & HOMICIDES
ASSAILANTS, ASPHALT & ALIBIS
VALLEYS, VEHICLES & VICTIMS
SUNSETS, SABBATICAL AND SCANDAL
TENTS, TRAILS AND TURMOIL
KICKBACKS, KAYAKS, AND KIDNAPPING
GEAR, GRILLS & GUNS
EGGNOG, EXTORTION, AND EVERGREEN
ROPES, RIDDLES, & ROBBERIES
PADDLERS, PROMISES & POISON
INSECTS, IVY, & INVESTIGATIONS
OUTDOORS, OARS, & OATH
WILDLIFE, WARRANTS, & WEAPONS
BLOSSOMS, BBQ, & BLACKMAIL
LANTERNS, LAKES, & LARCENY
JACKETS, JACK-O-LANTERN, & JUSTICE
SANTA, SUNRISES, & SUSPICIONS
VISTAS, VICES, & VALENTINES
ADVENTURE, ABDUCTION, & ARREST
RANGERS, RVS, & REVENGE

BOOKS BY TONYA

CAMPFIRES, COURAGE & CONVICTS
TRAPPING, TURKEY & THANKSGIVING
GIFTS, GLAMPING & GLOCKS
ZONING, ZEALOTS, & ZIPLINES
HAMMOCKS, HANDGUNS, & HEARSAY
QUESTIONS, QUARRELS, & QUANDARY
WITNESS, WOODS, & WEDDING
ELVES, EVERGREENS, & EVIDENCE
MOONLIGHT, MARSHMALLOWS, & MANSLAUGHTER
BONFIRE, BACKPACKS, & BRAWLS

Killer Coffee Cozy Mystery Series

Welcome to the Bean Hive Coffee Shop where the gossip is just as hot as the coffee.

SCENE OF THE GRIND
MOCHA AND MURDER
FRESHLY GROUND MURDER
COLD BLOODED BREW
DECAFFEINATED SCANDAL
A KILLER LATTE
HOLIDAY ROAST MORTEM
DEAD TO THE LAST DROP
A CHARMING BLEND NOVELLA (CROSSOVER WITH MAGICAL CURES MYSTERY)
FROTHY FOUL PLAY
SPOONFUL OF MURDER
BARISTA BUMP-OFF
CAPPUCCINO CRIMINAL
MACCHIATO MURDER

Holiday Cozy Mystery Series

CELEBRATE GOOD CRIMES!

FOUR LEAF FELONY
MOTHER'S DAY MURDER
A HALLOWEEN HOMICIDE
NEW YEAR NUISANCE
CHOCOLATE BUNNY BETRAYAL
FOURTH OF JULY FORGERY
SANTA CLAUSE SURPRISE
APRIL FOOL'S ALIBI

Kenni Lowry Mystery Series

Mysteries so delicious it'll make your mouth water and leave you hankerin' for more.

FIXIN' TO DIE
SOUTHERN FRIED
AX TO GRIND
SIX FEET UNDER
DEAD AS A DOORNAIL
TANGLED UP IN TINSEL
DIGGIN' UP DIRT
BLOWIN' UP A MURDER
HEAVENS TO BRIBERY

Magical Cures Mystery Series

Welcome to Whispering Falls where magic and mystery collide.

A CHARMING CRIME
A CHARMING CURE
A CHARMING POTION (novella)
A CHARMING WISH

A CHARMING SPELL
A CHARMING MAGIC
A CHARMING SECRET
A CHARMING CHRISTMAS (novella)
A CHARMING FATALITY
A CHARMING DEATH (novella)
A CHARMING GHOST
A CHARMING HEX
A CHARMING VOODOO
A CHARMING CORPSE
A CHARMING MISFORTUNE
A CHARMING BLEND (CROSSOVER WITH A KILLER COFFEE
COZY)
A CHARMING DECEPTION

Mail Carrier Cozy Mystery Series

Welcome to Sugar Creek Gap where more than the mail is being delivered.

STAMPED OUT
ADDRESS FOR MURDER
ALL SHE WROTE
RETURN TO SENDER
FIRST CLASS KILLER
POST MORTEM
DEADLY DELIVERY
RED LETTER SLAY

About Tonya

Tonya has written over 100 novels, all of which have graced numerous bestseller lists, including the USA Today. *Best known for stories charged with emotion and humor and filled with flawed characters, her novels have garnered reader praise and glowing critical reviews. She lives with her husband and a very spoiled rescue cat named Ro. Tonya grew up in the small southern Kentucky town of Nicholasville. Now that her four boys are grown men, Tonya writes full-time in her camper she calls her SHAMPER (she-camper).*

Learn more about her be sure to check out her website tonyakappes.com. Find her on Facebook, Twitter, BookBub, and Instagram

Sign up to receive her newsletter, where you'll get free books, exclusive bonus content, and news of her releases and sales.

If you liked this book, please take a few minutes to leave a review now! Authors (Tonya included) really appreciate this, and it helps draw more readers to books they might like. Thanks!